Joyce

Prudence, I know I'm paying more for Katherine's bond than I should.

Is your father in financial trouble? Is that why he insisted we marry?"

"No, not that I'm aware." Prudence looked down at her lap and played with the material of her dress. "He forced you to marry me because he doesn't believe any man would want me."

"That's nonsense. You're a beautiful woman."

"Who speaks her thoughts when women should keep silent."

"Look," he said as he lifted her chin with his forefinger, "I know what your father says about women and money, but he doesn't speak for all men. Some of us appreciate a woman with a good head on her shoulders."

Her heart started pounding. She took quick, short breaths. She searched his eyes, those wonderful green eyes. She wanted him to kiss her. Moving ever so slowly, she leaned toward him. And he leaned toward her. He slipped his gaze down to her lips and back to her eyes.

"Prudence, Urias, dinner is ready," Mrs. Campbell hollered from downstairs.

"Be right there," Urias answered. He finished replacing the bandage and took up the soiled strips.

Prudence sat like a boulder on the bed. What had just happened? Were they falling in love? No. . .she'd already fallen. But could Urias feel the same way? *Oh, dear Lord, help us understand what's happening.*

LYNN A. COLEMAN lives in North Central Florida with her husband of 31 years. She has three grown children and eight grandchildren. She is a minister's wife who writes to the Lord's glory. She founded American Christian Romance Writers, Inc. and served as president and advisor for the group. Lynn loves hearing from her readers. Visit her Web page at www.lynncoleman.com.

Books by Lynn A. Coleman

HEARTSONG PRESENTS
HP314—Sea Escape
HP396—A Time to Embrace
HP425—Mustering Courage
HP443—Lizzy's Hope
HP451—Southern Treasures
HP471—One Man's Honor
HP506—Cords of Love
HP523—Raining Fire

Hogtied

Lynn A. Coleman

Heartsong Presents

I'd like to dedicate this book to my granddaughter, Hannah Elizabeth. Having four older brothers will present some challenges in your life as well as a great blessing. All my love Hannah, and Grandma loves your beautiful smile.

A note from the Author:
I love to hear from my readers! You may correspond with me by writing:

> **Lynn A. Coleman**
> **Author Relations**
> **PO Box 719**
> **Uhrichsville, OH 44683**

ISBN 1-59310-490-1

HOGTIED

Our mission is to publish and distribute inspirational products offering exceptional value and biblical encouragement to the masses.

All scripture quotations are taken from the King James Version of the Bible.

All of the characters and events in this book are fictitious. Any resemblance to actual persons, living or dead, or to actual events is purely coincidental.

PRINTED IN THE U.S.A.

Or check out our Web site at www.heartsongpresents.com

one

Jamestown, Kentucky, 1840

"Urias, please reconsider."

"Mom, I've prayed. I've got to go."

Dad came up beside her and massaged her shoulders. "You go, Son. Do what you have to do; but remember, we'll need you in time for the spring planting."

"Yes, sir. You two mean the world to me. I promise I'll be back." Mom and Dad MacKenneth had opened their home to him seven years ago. They'd become his family, and he now looked differently on life.

Pamela MacKenneth stepped toward him and wrapped her arms around him. Urias embraced her tenderly. "I promise, if I can't find her this year, I'll leave her in the Lord's hands and trust that she's all right."

"I understand. I'll miss you terribly. Don't forget to say good-bye to Grandma and Grandpa," she encouraged.

"You think I'd be able sit again if I didn't say good-bye to them?" His adopted parents laughed. *Well, that helped lighten the mood a little,* Urias mused.

"Did you pack all the items we went over, Son?" his father asked.

"Yeah. Thanks for all the help."

"You know I would love to be hiking up those mountains with you."

He knew all too well. His father loved the mountains, but he loved his family more. When Urias had first met up with

Pam and Nash "Mac" MacKenneth, they'd been working their way through the Cumberland Gap area along the Wilderness Road. Somehow it seemed far more than seven years ago. Grandpa Mac had an accident, and Urias's adopted father took over the cares of the family farm. Of course, he and Mom weren't married at that time, and it took a bit before Dad came to his senses and asked her to marry him. But he finally had, and now they were a family of six— including Urias.

But Urias needed to find his first family now. He'd heard rumors that his younger sister was living in the Hazel Green area around Mount Sterling. He'd gone last year and hadn't found her. In 1837, Urias and his family had attended an Association at Hardshell Baptist Church. That's when he heard someone mention they once knew an O'Leary—and she had red hair just like him. Of course, red hair and Irish names seemed to go hand in glove. But he'd been searching for Katherine every fall right after the harvest ever since. This year he'd stay through the winter and give it one final look. It didn't matter that he'd given every merchant he met his name and a message as to how he could be reached in Jamestown.

Unfortunately, Jamestown was several days' travel from the Hazel Green area.

Sucking in a deep breath, Urias broke the merriment. "I gotta go. Pray for me."

"You know we will, Urias." Pam wiped the tears from her eyes.

Urias choked back his own. These two people loved him so much. He never felt anything less than a part of their family.

"Urias," Nash Jr. called out from behind him. Urias turned toward the young boy's voice.

"Hey, buddy, what ya got there?"

"A present." Urias remembered the first time he held Nash

when he was only a few hours old. It didn't seem possible that people could start out that small.

"Is it for me?" Setting his Kentucky long rifle against the wall, Urias knelt on one knee to put himself at a more equal footing with the boy.

"Uh-huh." Nash handed it to him with a smile that lit up the small child's face. It was wrapped in a scrap of cloth he recognized Mom had been working on a few days before.

"Thank you." Urias opened the cloth and found an old arrowhead. "This is wonderful, Nash. Thank you."

"If your powder gets wet, you can use it to fight off a bear." Personally, Urias hoped he wouldn't have to fight off any bear, ever. The scars on Mac's back were enough of a warning to stay clear of those critters as much as humanly possible.

He reached out and ruffled the boy's thick black hair. It was so much like his father's. "I'll remember that."

Dad winked.

Mom held back a chuckle at the boy's naïveté.

When the MacKenneths and Urias first met, he had a minor run-in with a bear. Thankfully, it was more interested in their ham than in them.

"Urias," his sisters said in unison. Molly, the older of the two, smiled. Her first two adult teeth were just beginning to show in the empty space. Sarah was two years younger than Molly, but she kept trying to wiggle her front teeth, hoping they'd come out soon like her big sister's had. Molly had long, dark, curly hair like her father. Sarah had straight brown hair like her mother.

Molly held a hand-wrapped package with a bow around it. "We made these for you."

"They're your favorite," Sarah added.

"Thank you, ladies. They smell wonderful," he said as he took the bundle of cookies and placed it in his pack.

He hugged and kissed each of his siblings, said his good-byes, and headed to his grandparents' house. He and Mac had built it after Grandpa Mac's accident—a single story, with ramps to go in and out of the place. Grandpa had been in a wheelchair for seven years, and Grandma tended to his every need. She also attended to Urias's education. After a brief but cheery good-bye, he headed out on horseback toward the mountains. "Lord, please let me find Katherine this time."

&

"Kate," Prudence called as she entered the darkened barn. She'd seen her retreat there once before. "Kate," she called once again.

"Pru?"

"Yes, it's me. Where are you?" Prudence blinked as her eyes adjusted to the lack of sunlight.

"Up here in the loft," Kate whispered.

Prudence climbed up the rustic ladder and saw Kate sitting there with her knees up to her chest. "Are you all right?"

Kate closed her eyes and her gorgeous red curls—which Prudence had envied more than once—bobbed as she nodded.

Prudence knelt in front of Kate and pushed those lovely locks from her friend's face, exposing the most beautiful green eyes one could wish for. But something overshadowed the beauty she'd seen in this servant gal. "You've been crying. What's the matter?"

"Nothing. I'm sorry." Kate wiped the tears from her face with the hem of her gray cotton dress. "What do you need?"

"I don't need a thing. I was looking for you. Now tell me why you've been crying."

Father had purchased Kate from a traveling salesman a couple of years prior. Kate never talked of her past, and Prudence wasn't sure she wanted to hear about it, either. Servants weren't always treated well, and slaves were treated worse. Kate wasn't a slave, but Father paid her no wages, and she had no freedom to up and leave. Father called her a bond servant, saying that once she worked off the price of her bond, she would be free to go. But he'd never said what that debt was—not that he ever had a mind to discuss private financial matters with the women in the family. Mother preferred it that way. Prudence, on the other hand, wanted to know. She'd listen in the shadows, over-hearing Father's business deals. Many times he'd make a profit. But Prudence knew her interest was foolishness. No woman was allowed a place in business, no matter how quickly she could calculate the figures.

She'd snuck into her father's office more than once to try to find the papers regarding Kate, but she never came up with any. If only there was something she could do for this poor woman.

"No, Miss Prudence. Pay me no never mind."

Prudence reached out and held her friend. "Please tell me."

"Your father is thinking of selling my bond."

"No. You'll never pay off your bond if he sells you."

"I know, but I don't care. I've nothing to live for. I'm useless to anyone but to fix their meals and clean their house. I'll never be free to marry. I've been beaten since I was ten and my brother run away. Mother used to beat him. Once he was gone, she started on me. Then one day she came home and said she'd sold me to a man, and I was to keep my mouth shut and do what the man asked and not say a word about it."

"I'm so sorry." Prudence didn't have to ask what Kate would have been forced to do.

"Ain't your fault. This be the best house I've been in, in six years."

"I've got to do something. Father can't sell your bond to another. Perhaps he'll let me pay for it."

Kate's freckled face looked straight at her. "You have money?"

"No, but I know where I can get some. I'd have to disguise myself as a man, but I think I could pull it off. I know how men deal with business."

"Miss Prudence, that be too dangerous, and your pa wouldn't permit it."

It was true. He wouldn't. But she'd have to do something. *God, help me to help Kate. She needs to know she has value. It isn't her fault she's been thrown into a life of servitude.*

"Trust me, Kate. God will help me and help you."

"God doesn't like someone like me."

"Oh, fiddlesticks. He likes you just fine. You're a good woman, Kate. You've been my friend and confidant for two years. I'm indebted to you. I promise with all that I am, I'll do whatever it takes to release you from this bondage."

Prudence wrapped the frail woman in her arms. Kate ate little and she slept even less. Her pale skin seemed a tinge gray in recent days. If God didn't do something soon, she'd probably spend her whole life in bondage—and that wasn't a way for anyone to live or die. "I love you, Kate."

Fresh sobs raked over the worn and weak body of her friend. Kate was only seventeen years old, but she looked closer to thirty. Prudence shuddered to think what had happened to her before coming to live here. Kate would flinch at the slightest movement back then, nearly jumping a couple inches off the floor when anyone spoke to her. She'd clearly been abused by someone who'd owned her bond.

"You said you have a brother?" Perhaps she could try to find him.

Kate nodded and smiled. "He's four years older than me. He left home a year after Pa died. Ma beat him bad. . .broke his arm and jaw one night. After he healed, he ran. He told me I'd be fine because Ma liked me and had never struck me. But he didn't know I'd be the closest target."

"I'm sorry. What's his name? Perhaps I could find him."

"Urias. But I think he's dead." Kate turned and held her knees to her chest once again.

Prudence's hopes for finding Kate's brother were quickly dashed. It was up to her. Kate had no one else in this world. *Father God, how can I help?* she prayed.

ès

Five days later, Urias rode into Hardshell, Kentucky, and up to the only church in thirty miles. It was the same church where he and his family had attended the Association gathering three years before when he'd heard Katherine's name. The church was a log building covered with boards. He stepped inside onto the puncheon floor, the split logs smooth from use. At the moment, only the parson occupied the rectangular space where fence rails substituted for seats. It wasn't much compared to the church he and his family attended back in Jamestown, but it would stand the test of time, Urias reasoned.

"Parson Duff." Urias extended his hand.

The older man reached out his beefy hands, grasped Urias by his upper arms, and held them as though Urias were an old friend. "And how do I know you, son?"

"My family and I came to the Association back in '37. I don't reckon you would remember me. My name's Urias O'Leary. My parents are Mr. and Mrs. Nash MacKenneth from Jamestown," he said as Parson Duff released Urias's arms, then took his right hand.

The parson stood a couple inches shorter than Urias, but his presence seemed larger. A far-off look gathered in the man's eye, and a smile spread across his broad lips. "There were several folk out to the Association. Grand time, grand time. The Lord be praised." Parson Duff released Urias's hand and looked him straight in the eye. "What is it I can do for you, son?"

"I'm looking for my sister. I've spent the past three years searching these hills, with no luck."

"And who might your sister be?"

"Her name is Katherine. Katherine O'Leary, unless she married. She's only seventeen, but in the hills—"

"The girls can be married at thirteen." Parson Duff finished his sentence.

Urias nodded. If Katherine was happily married, he'd stop worrying. But the growing sense of urgency to find her this year had made him wonder if she might actually be in danger.

"Come with me outside, son." Parson Duff led him out the front door of the church. "Can you describe her for me?"

"Apart from her having hair the same color as mine, we share the same green eyes. I don't know what she looks like beyond that. I left home seven years ago when I was fourteen. She was ten at the time."

The parson walked him over to his horse. "Fine animal."

"Thank you."

"Urias, there's a family over toward that there hollow whose son came for a good, long visit. Fine young man by the name of Shelton Greene. His father is a bit concerned about him. Now it ain't my place to say what Shelton is sufferin' from, but he did mention a gal named Kate with red hair and green eyes. I reckon if you go and see him, he could tell you if this Kate is your sister."

Urias's heart leapt for joy. Could it be this easy? Could he have found her on his first day? Every time in the past when he'd come to the church, the parson had not been around. "Thank you. Thank you so much." Urias jumped up on his horse and grasped the reins. He stopped for a moment. "Where can I find this man?"

Parson Duff chuckled and gave him simple directions. An

hour later, he'd met up with Shelton Greene.

"You say you're Kate's brother?" Shelton asked.

"I don't know. But I'd like to meet her. Is she here?"

The young man—all of sixteen he'd guess—looked down at his feet. "No. Kate is a bond servant to my father."

"A bond servant?"

"My father bought her two years ago. She has to work for him until her debt is paid in full."

"And how much does she owe your father?" Urias couldn't believe his sister had become a bond servant.

"Don't know. Father keeps his business dealings close to his chest. If you don't mind me asking, can you afford to buy her bond?"

No matter what the price, if it was his sister, he'd pay it. How could this have happened? Poor Katherine. He should have tried harder to find her years ago. Dad would have helped him. "I'll find a way."

Shelton gave him directions to Hazel Green and the Greene plantation. "Thank you. I'm much obliged."

Urias mounted his horse. *Had Mother been worse on Katherine? Dear God, please let this woman be her. And enable me to negotiate with her owner.*

He could spend the winter trapping. Perhaps that would bring in enough. Urias gave the horse a gentle prod with his heels. "Yah!" he ordered.

The winter would mean more months his sister would have to remain in another person's possession. Urias shuddered at the thought. No man should own another. Urias set his jaw. His nostrils flared. He couldn't get to Hazel Green fast enough. "Yah!" He snapped his whip above the horse's head.

two

Prudence spent the better part of the night working on possible ways to purchase Kate's bond. The greater problem would be to convince Father to let her buy it. His way of thinking, that women do not belong in business, was totally without merit in Prudence's opinion. But alas, the entire world seemed to feel that way. Prudence had never fit. Today was no exception.

She tapped on the oak door to his office. "Father," she called.

"Prudence." He beamed as he opened the door.

That's a good sign. Prudence took a step into the inner sanctum of his domain. "I wish to speak with you on a matter of importance, if you can spare a moment."

"For you my darling, anything."

Her heart beat wildly. "I'd like to speak with you on a business matter."

Hiram Greene instantly sobered. "Daughter, when are you going to accept the fact that business is not a matter to worry your precious little head over?"

"This is precious to me. It regards Kate. I wish to purchase her bond."

"Nonsense. She works for us presently. There is no need for you to purchase her."

"But, Father, I want to give Kate her freedom."

"Child, she'll have her freedom when she pays off her bond."

"When will that be?"

He looked down at his desk and started to fiddle with some

14

papers. "These matters are hard to understand. Trust me; I shall deal fairly with her debt."

"Is selling her, when her debt is nearly paid off, fair to her?" Prudence challenged.

Her father's face brightened with a shade of red she'd rarely seen. "I will not have you questioning my decisions. You must stop this meddling in men's affairs. I'll never find an appropriate suitor for you if you keep this up. Now, go discuss this with your mother. Perhaps she can put some common sense into you."

Prudence stomped out of her father's office, balling her hands into fists. If she didn't hold her tongue, Kate's debt could be worsened. She probably should have talked with her mother to begin with. Mother could persuade Father to do some things. Precious few, Prudence admitted. "Mother," she called.

"In my sewing room, Pru," she answered.

Their thirty-minute conversation proved fruitless, as well. Why couldn't she get her parents to see reason in this matter? And how could Kate know when her debt was paid if she didn't know how much it was? Father had been less than honest in some of his business deals. Prudence had seen the paperwork. But challenging him on this had been a huge mistake.

She left her mother's sewing room and sat on the front porch. The deep golds, yellows, and reds of the autumn leaves painted a gay feeling—unlike her own frustration.

A rider came up the road to the house. He sat tall in his saddle. Without getting off of his horse, he stopped and asked, "Would this be Hiram Greene's home?"

"Yes, sir. May I help you?"

"I need to speak with him on a business matter."

The tall stranger dismounted. Prudence got her first

glimpse of the man. He had red hair, freckles. . . "May I say who's calling?"

Kate was walking toward the front porch, her head down.

"Urias O'Leary."

"Urias?" Kate squealed and Prudence questioned.

Urias turned to the voice behind him. "Katherine?" He ran to her and swept her into his arms. "It is you." A lump the size of the Kentucky hills stuck in his throat. Tears filled Katherine's green eyes. He held her close, hugging her tight. "I've been looking for you for years. I'm so sorry. How are you? Are you all right? Where have you been?"

Katherine pushed herself from his arms and looked down at the ground. "I'm a servant of Mr. Greene's."

"I've come to get you, Katherine. I won't take no for an answer." He could feel the heat of his temper begin to rise. He slowly counted his blessings. *One, I've found Katherine. Thank You, Lord. Two, she's alive and safe. Thank You, Lord. Three. . .* "I can't believe I've found you."

"Nor I," Katherine replied through a halfhearted smile.

He thought she'd be more excited to see him. He turned back to the lady of the house. "May I speak with Mr. Greene?" he asked.

"I'll let him know you are here."

The brown-haired, petite lady scurried into the house. Urias turned his attention back to his sister and asked, "Did Mother sell you?"

She nodded yes.

"Katherine." He lifted her chin with his forefinger. "I'm sorry I took so long. I went back the following year, but you and Mother had moved. I've been looking for you ever since. What happened?"

"My daughter says you are Kate's brother." Hiram Greene stood all of five feet five inches, if Urias was any judge of a man's height. At six feet, he would easily tower over the older gentleman, but Mr. Greene stood on the top step and Urias remained on the ground with a half dozen steps between them.

"Yes, sir. May I take her home with me?"

"Now, Mister. . . ?"

"O'Leary," Urias supplied.

"Mr. O'Leary, I'm a businessman, and I can't be letting my help run off with any man that comes along. How can you prove to me she is your sister?"

Is the man blind? We both have the same hair and eye color and obviously have similar features. "You have my word."

Hiram Greene chuckled. "Come into my office, son. Let's see what we can work out."

Urias gave a parting glance to his sister, then followed the man into his two-story mansion. The front room opened into an entryway larger than the living room in his parents' spacious farmhouse. Urias wondered how long he'd have to work before he could earn enough to purchase his sister's freedom. It was apparent, without Hiram Greene saying a word, he would not simply hand her over. And he would be far less likely to release her with nothing more than Urias's promise to pay off her debt. But Urias determined to plead his case.

"Mr. Greene," Urias began upon entering the gentleman's office.

"Mr. O'Leary," Hiram Greene interrupted. "Please take a seat. May I call you Urias?"

Urias nodded.

"Fine, fine. Urias, I'm not above selling Kate's bond."

"Sir, if I may be so bold, I have little funds with me. But I can give you my word I will return to my home and come back with the appropriate funds. How much is my sister's bond?"

"Now, now, before we talk figures, I would need to calculate how much it is. As to the matter of your leaving and returning, that will be fine. But your sister will remain with us until the debt is paid."

Urias thought for a moment. If she'd been with the family for two years, what would be the problem?

"However, I must tell you, I've had another offer to purchase Kate's bond."

"What? You can't sell her. She's my sister." Urias knew he should keep his anger in check, but there were some things a man just couldn't stomach, and ever since hearing of his sister being sold into servitude, it had been souring something terrible.

"I'm a reasonable man, Mr. O'Leary, but the hour is late, and I'd need something more than your word of your return to consider your offer over that of another."

Urias suspected the man was just trying to up his price. "How much?"

※

Prudence leaned closer to the back wall of the coat closet. Sequestered in her hiding place, she could hear just about everything that went on in her father's business negotiations. Urias O'Leary was not pleased to see his sister in such a condition and, for that matter, neither was Prudence. Something had changed over the past couple of months with Kate—she seemed more despondent. At this time last year, she had sported a healthy tan. Now Kate's coloring was pasty, at best.

"Five hundred dollars," her father replied to Urias's third request to know just exactly how much would be needed to meet his sister's bond.

"Five hundred dollars?" Urias reached into his pocket. "I have twenty."

Her father let out a wicked laugh.

"A hundred and a fine steed. Would you take it and let me return with the rest?" Urias pushed.

She could just see her father rubbing his chin as he always did, sitting back in his chair behind the desk. "If I take your horse, how long would it take you to return?"

"It was five days on horseback, so possibly a month."

"Fine, a month and five hundred dollars, and you'll be able to purchase your sister's indebtedness. The horse stays here as collateral. The sun is setting, Urias. Have dinner with us, and you may spend the night in the barn."

"Thank you, but I won't impose."

Prudence leaned against the back wall. *Five hundred dollars! No wonder Father wouldn't let me pay the debt.*

"May I visit with my sister?"

"After her chores are finished, which will be after our dinner is served and she's cleaned up the dishes. You're welcome to have dinner with us."

"No, thank you."

Prudence couldn't blame him for not wanting to create more work for his sister. Little did he know that Kate was only one of three in the kitchen.

"The barn is yours for the night, if you wish," her father once again extended his offer.

Words were mumbled, and Prudence couldn't make them out.

She had some money in her room, she knew, but not that much. *Think, Pru, think.* Then it hit her—Thomas Hagins was selling some hogs. If Urias herded them down to the Cumberland Gap, he could turn a profit. The question was: Would Mr. Hagins take Urias's word, unlike her father? And would Urias want to herd hogs? A mental flash of Urias following a herd of large hogs through the windy foothills to the Cumberland went through her mind.

She slithered out of the coat closet and waited in the front room for Urias to leave her father's office. She had to help him. Kate needed to be free. She needed to live once again. Prudence thought back on what Kate had spoken of yesterday about her life as a bond servant, about her mother, and even her brother. The abuse had to end. If Pru couldn't convince her father to give her Kate's bond, then she'd do what it would take to help Urias purchase it.

Urias stomped out of her father's office but refrained from slamming the door. His temper showed by the redness of his face.

"Mr. O'Leary," Prudence whispered as he passed by. "Meet me in the barn. I have an idea to help free your sister."

"What? Who are you?"

"Prudence Greene. Your sister is my best friend. I want to help."

He set his hat upon his head. "A friend doesn't. . ." He stopped short of completing his comment.

Prudence figured she knew what the man was going to say, but now was not the time or the place to be discussing such matters. Her father would have her head if he found her discussing business one more time. Mother had already threatened to send her east to some high society fashion school for ladies. Thankfully, Father had talked her out of that for the time being.

"The barn, Mr. O'Leary." She hurried up the stairs, praying her father hadn't heard her brief discussion with Urias. At the top of the stairs, she turned down the hall and down the back stairs, sneaking out the back door to the barn. It was the long way to go, but the best way when you didn't want to be intercepted. The barn door creaked as she opened it. The smell of fresh hay and oats wafted past her nose. "Urias?" she called. "Are you in here?"

The door creaked open again, letting in some golden light from the sunset. Prudence ducked behind the tack wall. The tall, thin frame of Urias O'Leary was highlighted in a dark silhouette. He led his horse by the reins into the barn. "Come on, boy, you'll have a comfortable home for a while."

Urias O'Leary was a handsome man, and he seemed to have a peace about him in the way he handled himself.

He stroked the horse's head. "I'll be back for you as soon as I can, boy."

"Urias," Prudence called.

Urias spun in the air and pointed his rifle straight at her.

"It's me. Prudence."

He lowered his weapon.

"Tell me what you must, woman. I need to be on my way."

"I have an idea," Prudence said.

≈

Urias sat on a rail and listened. She had an interesting plan, he had to admit, and he certainly knew the Cumberland Gap area. From here down to the Wilderness Road would be a trick, though. He'd have to get some detailed directions. The big question was whether he would be able to purchase five hundred hogs with only some of the money down. Would this Thomas Hagins trust him more than Hiram Greene did?

"Your plan has merit, but. . ."

"I know. But would Thomas extend the note to be paid upon your return."

"Precisely."

"I could give Thomas my word."

The petite woman did not appear frail; she seemed like she could take on the world, given the right incentive. "Would he believe you?"

"I don't rightly know. Men don't like women talking business."

He wouldn't argue the point, but he'd long since learned from his adopted mom that women could have as much of a head for numbers as a man and quite possibly a better head from time to time. Urias didn't have five hundred dollars for Katherine's bond, and while his parents might have enough, the question still remained how he'd manage to pay them back. He could spend the winter furring, but that would only bring in some of it. But it would be worth it—anything to get Katherine out of a life of servitude. On the other hand, Prudence's idea would bring a quicker income in less than a month's time.

"Urias, I do love your sister. She's become like a sister to me. But we must act quickly. I found Kate crying in the barn yesterday. Apparently the subject of her being sold again had come up. I tried to purchase her bond from Father myself, but he wouldn't listen to me. He knew I would simply forgive her the debt, and it just reinforced his thought that a woman had no sense of business. Perhaps he's right. I can't see the logic in one man owning another or, in your sister's case, owing a debt that seems never to be paid up."

"My mother never would have sold Katherine for five hundred dollars." He jumped off the rail. "Don't get me wrong. She would have sold Katherine, but she would have sold her cheap. I don't understand how the bill could be so high."

Prudence sighed. "I don't know the nature of your sister's debt to my father. But I do know he would charge her for her food and clothing."

"But he doesn't pay her a wage."

"Precisely. That would keep her forever in his debt."

Urias kicked up some hay from the barn's floor. *Lord, I'm upset here. Calm me down so I don't do or say something foolish,* he prayed.

"Urias." Prudence placed her hand on his shoulder. He

turned to her. He could see the tears in her eyes. She truly did care for Katherine and her well-being. His heart softened.

"I'm not angry with you. Truthfully, I'm more upset with myself. I never should have left without bringing Katherine with me."

"You were merely a boy at the time. How could you have cared for her?"

"I would have found a way. And I know Mom and Dad would have taken her in just as they took me in, if she were with me at the time."

"One can't look back and change things. We have to decide what to do now. I'm worried about her. Kate's not looking well. I think she's lost the will to live." Prudence began to cry. "We must help her."

Urias wrapped the woman in a compassionate embrace. "God will help us."

"Amen." She sniffled.

"Get your hands off my daughter!" Hiram Greene bellowed.

three

Urias released Prudence and jumped back.

"How dare you!" Hiram Greene's eyes bulged. His entire face resembled that of a setting sun.

"Father, it isn't what you think!" Prudence cried.

"Get into the house!" Hiram ordered.

"But, Father, Urias. . ."

"Urias, is it?" The older man fumed. "Get to the house, now, before I take a switch to you."

Urias's hackles went up. "Nothing improper happened."

Hiram faced Urias. "Don't you be telling me what is what, boy. I have a mind to send you packing."

"Daddy!" Prudence cried.

"Get!" He pointed to the open barn door.

Urias chastised himself for not having shut the door when he entered. He knew Prudence had planned on meeting him in the barn. And he knew it was not socially correct for a man and woman to meet privately. He hadn't thought about that. He'd only been thinking about his sister and how hard it was going to be to get her out of this servant lifestyle.

"Sir, if I could explain."

"I don't think there is a thing you can say that will placate me in this situation." Hiram scrutinized Urias's horse. He relaxed his shoulders and asked, "Is he fast?"

Urias nodded. He didn't know what to say at the abrupt change in Hiram's demeanor. He'd never met a man who behaved quite like this before.

"Does he have papers?"

"No. I bred him from one of my father's mares and a wild horse I captured."

"Hmm." Hiram went over to the horse. "He has good lines."

"Yes, sir." What else could Urias say? How could this man be so belligerent one moment, then congenial the next?

"You'll spend the night in the barn. If you leave, I'll call the law on you. I need to speak with my wife on the matter of your inappropriate actions with my daughter."

"Nothing—"

Hiram held up his hand. "I'm not interested in what you have to say, son. You're a stranger to me and so is your kin. Your word means nothing. Have I made myself clear?"

"Yes, sir."

"Good. Supper will be in thirty minutes. I'll send Kate out with a plate for you."

"Yes, sir." Urias stepped up to his horse and loosened the saddle.

Hiram Greene marched out of the barn, then turned back around at the doorway. "Fine-looking horseflesh. Mighty fine."

Urias knew horses, and he knew Bullet could run like the wind. He'd been offered a fair dollar a time or two for the steed. But he'd always held back from selling him. He'd been considering purchasing his own place to raise horses. Horse-racing was beginning to be big business in Kentucky, and a man could do well breeding prime stock for the competition.

Hiram Greene, on the other hand, had the wealth of high society, while his business negotiations seemed more like wrestling a pig out of the mud. Urias felt certain he was paying more than his sister's bond. But what did it matter? He'd buy her freedom.

Urias finished removing the horse's tack and put him in an empty stall with some fresh oats. He groomed the animal; it had been days since he'd had a good brushing. He'd just finished cleaning up when his sister came in with a plate of food.

"What did you do, Urias? The house is in an uproar."

"Nothing," he grumbled.

"I don't think I've ever seen Mr. Greene this angry before. Prudence is in tears. The missus is beside herself." Katherine sat down beside him. "You be a bit of a handful, Urias. Seems little has changed."

She had grown into a fine-looking woman—no longer the thin little girl with huge front teeth and pigtails. "My life is good, Katherine. I'm going to get you out of here. I promise."

"Where have you been?" she asked, handing him his plate.

"For the first six months, I ran from spot to spot. I barely had much to eat, except for the food I could catch. My hunting skills back then left a wee bit to be desired. I found a barn I could hide in, and I was staying in there when I met Mom and Dad."

"Mom and Dad? Father's been dead for nearly nine years."

"I'm sorry. Mac and Pam MacKenneth took me in and made me a part of their family."

Katherine looked down at the floor.

"Katherine, we've searched for years. When we returned the following fall, no one knew where you and Mom went off to."

"Mom sold me by then. I don't know where she is. She took the money and run, I guess."

His mother was a horrid woman, but never in his wildest dreams would he have suspected she would sell her child for profit. "How could she sell you?"

"I don't want to talk about it."

"I'm sorry."

"I wish ya'd found me sooner," she whispered.

The lump of potatoes stuck in his throat. He forced it

down. "I tried, Katherine. I've been looking for you for six years. Unfortunately, we only had a short period of time in which to do our searching. So every fall we'd return to the area and ask people questions. Three years ago, at a revival down in Hardshell, we heard there was a gal fitting your general description who was a servant in someone's house. So I've been concentrating up here. I met up with Shelton Greene in Hardshell, and he told me where you were and how I could find you."

"Are you able to buy my bond?"

"I will. I have to go home and borrow the money from my parents, but somehow I will buy it, Katherine. I promise you won't have to stay here too long."

"It hasn't been a bad place to work," she mumbled.

Urias reached over and placed his hand on her arm. "Katherine, I'm sorry you've gone through all of this. I should have taken you with me."

Tears welled in his sister's green eyes. Urias could feel the same happening in his own.

"I'll pack my bags." She stood to leave.

"Katherine, I can't take you with me. Mr. Greene does not trust me. My word means nothing to him."

Katherine nodded. "Very well," she droned, her words reaching down to the pit of his stomach. Urias doubted he had ever seen a person this depressed before. He couldn't leave his sister here much longer. She needed rescuing, and, thank God, he'd been sent to rescue her.

"I love you, Katherine. You've never stopped being in my prayers."

"Prayers?" Her eyes flickered like fire and her face flushed. "Prayers are worthless."

❧

Prudence couldn't believe her ears. Her parents had been

arguing for the better part of an hour. Not a morsel of food had been touched on either of their plates. Father insisted she had disgraced the family and must be married immediately. Mother felt marriage was a bit extreme. Finishing school was Mother's answer, and had been for the better part of a year.

Urias O'Leary might also feel marriage a bit extreme, Prudence guessed. What had she done by meeting with him? *Dear Lord, please intervene.*

Prudence left the table and dining room as quietly as possible. Her parents weren't talking with her—just about her and around her. She felt fairly certain Mother could talk Father out of a forced wedding, which she had no interest in participating in. But should she warn Urias? The only way would be to go out to the barn. Kate hadn't come back in from her visit with her brother. Prudence pondered for a moment, hesitating in the hallway. If she went out to the barn, Father would be furious enough that no matter what reasoning power Mother had, it would be useless. She chose the stairs and the solitude of her bedroom.

In her room, Prudence prayed. She opened her money box and removed what little savings she had. Eighteen years old and not yet pledged in marriage—it had been a source of contention in her home since her sixteenth birthday. Women in the hills of Kentucky were married at thirteen or fourteen, and Prudence was rapidly approaching her spinster years. But marriage should be more than an arrangement between her father and some business partner's son. At least, she'd always hoped and prayed it would be. She wanted love. Someone who loved her more than her father's money.

Oddly enough, when Father began spouting off her need to marry Urias, the possibility hadn't seemed completely intolerable. He was a handsome man, and a girl could get lost looking into those marvelous green eyes. Prudence shook off the thought. She wouldn't be forced into marrying for simply talking with a man. They'd done nothing wrong. Fortunately, she had found a brief moment to explain to her mother what had transpired before her father came in the house, ranting and raving.

But something wasn't right about the price of Kate's bond. Father would never pay that kind of money even on a good horse, much less for a servant. But why would he overcharge Katherine's brother? He'd always been a fair man in business. But recently he'd been making some strange decisions—from what little she had heard in the closet beside his office. *I really must stop eavesdropping*, she reminded herself for the hundredth time.

She really didn't care about knowing the personal details of other people's lives. She merely wanted to understand the workings of finance. For some reason, it had always piqued her interest, even as a small child.

Wrapping her small savings into a handkerchief, she set it aside to have Kate bring out to Urias. Sitting down at her writing desk, she penned a brief note to him, letting him know the monies were to purchase additional hogs. She blew the ink gently to finish off the drying, folded it neatly, and placed it inside the folds of the handkerchief, then scurried down the hallway to the rear of the house to the servants' quarters.

"Kate," she whispered, tapping the door.

No answer. She turned the crystal knob and pushed the door open. Kate wasn't in her room. Prudence worked her way down the back stairway to the kitchen. Again, no Kate. *Where could she be?*

Prudence heard her parents still discussing their problem of what to do with their daughter. Sometimes Prudence wondered if she'd been born into the wrong family. Kate had to be in the barn with Urias.

Taking in a deep breath, she hurried out to the barn and prayed she wouldn't get caught. She didn't enter but stepped in the doorway and called out to Kate.

"She's not here," Urias answered.

"Do you know where I might find her?" Prudence asked. "Urias, I have something for you. I'm leaving it wrapped in a white handkerchief by the door. I can't come in or Father would be beside himself. You should be warned; he's planning on us getting married."

"What?" Urias popped out of the dark shadows of the barn. "I'll not stand for it."

The sharp response hurt, even though she knew Urias was right. The idea was ridiculous. "Mother is trying to convince him to send me off to finishing school. Please take this. It's a little more to help you buy more hogs."

"Prudence, I have not decided whether or not to purchase the hogs."

"But?" Prudence stepped closer to the door and to Urias.

"I cherish my parents' counsel, and I've been praying and thinking I should speak with them. But if I leave my horse to insure my return, that will take weeks. I simply don't know what to do. Katherine doesn't trust me. I don't know if I can blame her. She didn't say anything but. . ."

"Oh, Urias." She stepped forward and placed her hand on his forearm. "You have to give her time. She's had a rough life, and you seem to have had a good one."

He squeezed his eyes shut. "I should never have left her with our mother."

"You were a boy. Don't be—"

"So hard on myself? That's the problem. I was only thinking of myself. I never thought what my mother would have done. She was a drunk and she beat me. Of course she'd beat

Katherine once I was gone. I never looked beyond myself. This is all my fault."

"No. I can't believe that. I don't know you, but a child can't be responsible for an adult's actions. You weren't responsible for your mother beating you any more than you're responsible for your mother beating Kate." *How can I get through to this man?* "Stop thinking on the past, Urias. Kate needs you now. You're here now. Take this." She handed him the handkerchief. "It's all I have at the moment."

His fingers brushed hers as he reached for the proffered gift. A flash of heat shot through her like a bolt of lightning.

"That settles it!" her father shouted from the back stairs of the house.

"Settles what?" Urias whispered.

"Our marriage." Prudence blushed.

Dear God in heaven, help me, Urias prayed.

"Prudence Greene, get in this house this moment!" Hiram Greene shouted for all to hear.

The barn began to spin. Urias grabbed the rail to stabilize himself. This couldn't be happening. *No one would force someone to marry for simply speaking with another. It wasn't legal, was it?*

Urias stuffed the handkerchief in his pocket as he watched Prudence walk toward her father. Her shoulders drooped farther with each step closer. The man was a tyrant, or so it would seem. *If he treats his own daughter this way, how does he treat Katherine?* Urias closed his eyes and tried to keep his mind from thinking the worst.

"Mr. O'Leary, come to my office," Hiram ordered.

If ever a man needed divine inspiration and wisdom, it was now. *Lord, I am up against a post here. Prudence says her father is going to insist on us getting married. I can't do that. I need Your help and guidance.*

Urias dusted off his pants and walked toward the front

door. He couldn't leave this plantation soon enough. But first he had to get something in writing concerning Katherine's bond and the agreement he had with her owner. Then he'd shake the dust from his heels faster than any disciple leaving an unholy city.

He walked into the house and straight into Hiram Greene's office. There he waited, counting time by the construction of a small spider web in the upper right-hand corner of the brick fireplace. The sun had set, and a bracing coolness filled the house. *Perhaps it isn't only the weather,* he mused. Should he light a fire? Would it be considered neighborly or imposing?

Finally, he sat down in a fancy, hand-carved oak chair. He quieted his heart and prayed.

"Mr. O'Leary." Urias startled as Hiram Greene marched into his office. "I've called for the preacher, and you shall marry my daughter this evening."

Urias held down his temper. "With all due respect, Mr. Greene, I will not marry your daughter. We did nothing improper."

"You will marry my daughter, or I will not sell you your sister's bond. This is not negotiable, Mr. O'Leary." Hiram Greene sauntered across his office and sat down behind the desk as if he didn't have a care in the world.

"You can't do this. You can't force your daughter to marry me or me to marry your daughter. We had an agreement for my sister's bond."

"Yes, but that was before you dishonored me and my house by your indecent behavior with my daughter."

"I did no such thing!" Urias defended.

"I beg to differ, sir, and since I am the head of this household and I make the decisions here, that is my final decision. You will marry my daughter when the preacher arrives, or I'll have you thrown in jail." He leaned forward. "This is within my power and my right as a father."

Not only had he threatened to not sell Urias his sister's bond, now he threatened a jail sentence. If the circuit judge came around these parts as often as he did in Jamestown, Urias could be sitting behind bars for quite a while.

Urias heard a team of horses and a carriage coming up toward the house. "Preacher is here, son. What's it going to be?"

four

Prudence cried throughout the entire ceremony. The things her father had said to her were so hurtful, she didn't even want to think about them. He also told her that if she didn't go through with the wedding, he would sell Kate to someone else and put Urias in jail until the circuit judge came by—which, in Prudence's estimation, would be next spring. She had little choice but to stand beside Urias and repeat the vows the preacher performed.

Once the ceremony was over, Urias placed his hat upon his head and exited the house. Who could blame him? She certainly couldn't.

She ran up to her room and cried as she packed her bag.

"Prudence," her mother called from behind the door. "May I come in?"

Prudence didn't bother to answer. Since when did it matter to her parents what she wanted? Her mother entered the room. "Darling, look at the bright side—you have a husband."

Prudence narrowed her gaze on her mother.

"All right, maybe that was the wrong thing to say. But you're not getting any younger."

What little dignity Prudence had left flew out the window. Even her own mother thought the only way Prudence could get a husband was to be forced into a marriage. "This is not a marriage, Mother; it's a jail sentence."

"Maybe he isn't a bad sort."

What little she knew of Urias, he wasn't a bad sort at all.

He cared deeply for his sister, enough to persistently search for her for years.

Prudence opened her closet door and pulled out her carpetbag.

"What are you doing?"

"Packing. I'm married now. Don't I have to live with my husband?"

"But I thought you and he would live here."

Was her mother that oblivious? "Mom, he has a family, a job of his own."

"But your father said—"

"I don't know what Daddy said, but I know one thing; he cannot control Urias O'Leary. If he hadn't threatened Urias with the loss of his sister's freedom and jail time, I doubt he would have married me."

"Oh, my dear, I don't want you to leave. I'd hoped he'd move in with you."

"No, Mother, he has his own life. Somehow, I have to figure out a way to share it." *But not for long. There has to be a·way to have the marriage annulled.*

There was a knock at her open door. Prudence glanced over. Kate stood there, shaking. "Urias told me to tell you he'll be leaving in the morning and return as soon as he can with the money for your father."

"Thank you." Prudence sighed.

"See? He is a reasonable man. You can stop packing now." Her mother exited the room.

Prudence dumped the contents of her carpetbag out and began repacking. This time she packed for a wilderness journey. Her mother might be pleased with her staying, but Prudence needed to leave this house, and she needed to help earn Kate's freedom. Somehow, she and Urias would figure a way out of this foolish marriage. Then hopefully Prudence would find a place for herself in this world apart from her family—a place where people would accept and appreciate all of her hidden talents.

"Prudence," Kate whispered, "I'm sorry."

"Hush. This isn't your fault. It's my own. I shouldn't have gone to the barn a second time. I should have waited to find you to deliver the. . . What does it matter? It's over, it's done with, and now your brother is paying for my foolishness. I'm the one who is sorry."

"Can I help?" Kate asked.

"Thank you." Prudence grabbed the carpetbag and set it right side up on the bed once again. The handle came off in her hands. Fresh tears filled her eyes.

❧

Urias woke at the sound of the rooster's first crow. He rubbed the back of his stiff neck and moaned, then stood up and stretched. He doubted he'd ever had such a fitful night's sleep. Every hour he seemed to wake with the nightmare of the evening before. Married at the end of a pointed sword. Granted, there had been no blades present, but it certainly had felt like it.

All night he kept having this nagging feeling that something besides Hiram Greene's daughter's honor was at stake in this forced marriage. To threaten Katherine's freedom and jail time to mean the man didn't play fair in business. That realization only solidified Urias's original thought that the bond he'd agreed to pay was much higher than the debt his sister owed.

He reached for his saddle and proceeded to hitch Bullet up. Urias had decided somewhere around the middle of the night that since he'd been forced to marry Prudence, the original agreement for the purchase of his sister's bond was null and void. With Bullet, he could possibly make it back to Jamestown in three days. Time was of the essence now.

Hiram Greene was not a man to be trusted. If he would force his daughter to marry a stranger with no respect for her feelings, would he honor the agreement of selling off Katherine's bond? And now that Urias had found her, he wasn't about to lose her.

The barn door creaked open. Urias chastised himself again for not having closed it last evening when he rendezvoused with Prudence.

Prudence stood there with a hastily mended carpetbag in one hand and dressed for travel. Her brown hair was pulled back under a white cotton bonnet. She was a beautiful woman; he'd give her that. But no man should be forced to marry her. What was Hiram Greene's problem?

"Good morning," she said in a timid voice.

"Morning. Going somewhere?"

"With you," she replied and walked over to him.

"No, no. I agreed to marry you, but I'm not taking you with me," Urias stammered. "I mean, I'm not taking you with me to my parents' house." That didn't sound right, either.

She squared her shoulders and replied, "I'm your wife now."

"I'm well aware of that fact."

"What I mean to say is, I'm free to go with you and I want to help. With my help, we can herd the hogs to the Cumberland Gap in less time."

He had forgotten about her ingenious plan regarding raising the money himself. "I was planning on speaking with my parents and borrowing the money."

"How long would that take?" she asked.

"Eight days—ten at the most. The problem would be how fast we could get the funds."

She nodded. Urias knew—he wasn't sure how he knew—but he could tell she was conjuring up a scheme of some kind. "I'm not of a mind to tell you what to do, but for the same amount of time, we could probably herd some hogs down to the Cumberland Gap and back again."

The idea of not owing his parents five hundred dollars for his sister's bond was appealing. With the profit, he'd be able to buy his own property and start breeding horses.

"Even if we don't raise enough capital," she continued, "I'm certain we'd raise enough for Father to release Kate. Especially since we are married now."

Urias sunk his hands into his pockets and felt the folded handkerchief she'd given him the night before. He pulled it out and opened it. Inside he found some money and a note. Reading it, he realized once again how deeply this woman cared for his sister.

She reached over and placed her hand on his forearm. "Urias, please. Can we at least talk with Thomas Hagins and see if we can barter with him?"

"Have you ever lived on the road?" he asked. He continued to ready the horse for travel.

"No," she admitted. "I promise not to complain. Maybe it is my pride, but I resent what Father did last night. Besides, I need to leave this house, and our marriage gives me the opportunity to put distance between myself and my father."

He couldn't blame her there. If he'd been that man's child, he'd be livid, too. *Perhaps that's why Prudence's brother is staying with their uncle in Hardshell,* Urias mused. "All right. You can come. And, yes, we'll talk with Thomas Hagins. But if he won't work a deal, you return home, and I'll go to Jamestown to get the money needed. Agreed?"

"Thank you."

He glanced down at her ladies' heeled boots. "Do you have a more rugged pair of shoes?"

"No."

"Is there a place nearby where we can purchase you a pair?"

"There's a general store not too far from Thomas Hagins's place."

"Good." He reached for her bag to fasten it to the horse's saddle. "You'll ride; I'll walk. We'll get farther that way."

She nodded her agreement. Urias didn't know if this was the makings of a contrite spirit or whether the wealthy young woman had always expected such favors. It didn't matter; with those boots, they wouldn't get far.

He hoisted her into the saddle. A bolt of awareness shot through him. For the first time, he realized this beautiful woman was his wife, and there wasn't a thing he could do about it, one way or the other.

&

Prudence sat mesmerized in the saddle. Urias's touch had been so gentle and yet so full of power when he helped her up on the horse. If Father hadn't forced them to get married, would something have developed between them? She contemplated that the entire five-hour journey to Thomas Hagins's place. They talked little on the trip. For the most part, she just gave him directions. She didn't know what to think of Urias. One minute he seemed warm and compassionate; the next he was distant—almost cold. They had to find a way to annul the marriage. No one should be forced to live like this.

Of course, that was what Kate's life must have been like these many years—forced to live for the wishes of others. Forced to do things that were. . . Prudence stopped the thoughts. Kate had never said outright that she'd been abused by some of those who'd owned her bond. But something had happened to her—something that clearly made her feel unworthy to be considered equal with others.

Kate was why she was on this horse. Kate was the reason she'd stand up and give up her own life and her own happiness to save another from a life of servitude.

They walked up to the white-trimmed house of Thomas Hagins and knocked on the door.

"Miss Greene, what a pleasure to see you." Thomas Hagins extended his hand.

Prudence accepted it. "It's good to see you, Mr. Hagins. May I introduce my husband, Urias O'Leary?" Thomas Hagins's eyebrows shot up as his eyes widened. Did everyone think she was unfit to be a wife? "Urias, Mr. Hagins."

"Husband? My dear, it has been too long." Thomas shook Urias's hand.

"We've come to do business, sir. My wife and I would like to purchase some hogs to bring them to the Cumberland Gap. Prudence seems to believe there is a good profit there for a man."

"She's a right smart one. 'Tis true, I've made a dollar or two myself. Unfortunately, I no longer have the legs for the journey. Price is $1.25 per hundred pounds of hogs. How many do you want?"

"I've got a hundred on me, and I can leave my steed as a deposit. I was hoping you might be willing to let me purchase five hundred hogs and bring the money back to you after I return from the Gap."

"I don't know. That's asking an awful lot."

Prudence couldn't help herself. "Mr. Hagins, I realize you don't know my husband, but he is an honorable man." *After all, he married me.* "If my father thinks enough of Urias to give my hand in marriage to him, that should speak for something."

Thomas rubbed the day's growth on his chin.

"Let me look at the horse."

Urias looked up and winked. Prudence smiled. For the first time in her life, a man hadn't put her down for speaking her mind.

"Fine-looking steed. I'd be interested in buying him for the purchase of the hogs."

"He's yours if I fail to return with the money. But I need him. If I could trouble you for a mule to help carry our packs, that would be mighty fine of you. I'd be willing to pay for the animal," Urias offered.

"The horseflesh alone is worth more than the hogs. You've got yourself a deal, son." Thomas and Urias shook on it.

The men worked out the details while Prudence worked out some food supplies for the road with Mrs. Hagins. Urias had given her back the money she'd given to him yesterday. The Haginses put them up for the evening. Urias slept on the floor and gave the bed to Prudence. Neither one of them was ready to make the marriage complete, but it still stung to realize she was not wanted by her own husband. Prudence silently cried herself to sleep for the second night in a row.

five

Urias and Prudence woke early the next morning and ate the hot breakfast Mrs. Hagins had fixed for them. By six, they began herding the hogs toward the Cumberland Gap. Urias had spent the better part of the evening speaking with Thomas about hogs and how to best herd them. Before going to bed last night, he had fashioned a couple of willow switches to snap and prod the hogs forward.

By noon, they had covered only a couple of miles. At this rate, they wouldn't make the gap before snowfall. Frustrated, he sat down to the meal Prudence had prepared. "Thank you," he said, taking the offered dish from her hands.

"You're welcome. I purchased a few things from Mrs. Hagins last night to make our travels more comfortable."

"How are your feet?"

"I find the shoes quite comfortable. The two pairs of woolen socks seem a bit much, but I'm sure you're right about blisters from new shoes if I don't wear them."

"You may still get them. You can sit on the burro if you need to."

"Thank you. I'm all right." She looked down at her plate. His heart tightened once again, knowing what this marriage was doing to her.

"Urias, we're not moving fast enough, are we?"

"No, but I figure it will take a day or two to learn how to move the hogs forward."

Her face brightened.

"Once we've got them on the path and moving at a good

pace, we should make up for some of the lost time."

"How long before we hit the Wilderness Road?"

"Three days—possibly four." Urias finished off his meal. "Thank you." He handed her the empty plate. "I'll get the hogs moving while you clean up. They can feed along the way. There's a fresh water stream that should help the hogs recover from the journey. They won't eat much, but we don't want them to lose too many pounds before we get there.

"I'll keep my eye out for quail for dinner tonight. Do you like quail?" Urias asked.

"Yes. That would be nice. You'll have to teach me some about cooking on an open fire. I know a little, but precious little, I'm afraid."

Urias nodded. He couldn't fault her for her upbringing, and he knew there were some folks who lived in cities who didn't understand how to live off the land. But still, a woman should know how to cook. He thought back on his warm meal of beans with chunks of ham thrown in. *She knows how to cook some things,* he amended.

Urias picked up his long switch and started snapping it in the air above the hogs' heads. Instantly, they started to move. Down and around the curvy mountain trail they traveled until, five hours later, they arrived at the clearing Thomas Hagins had recommended.

As he settled the hogs in for the evening, he noticed Prudence silently making a campfire. *The quail.* He'd forgotten all about them. He'd been too focused on the swine and getting them to the field. He finished counting them and took off for the woods. With any luck, he'd find a couple quail before too long.

He examined the ground, looking for telltale signs of the bird. Generally, they nested on the ground. He looked for overturned leaves and scratching in the dirt. What he didn't expect to see was the large set of tracks to his left.

He glanced back at the camp. They were vulnerable. He'd have to stay awake the night to be on guard.

❧

"Bear?"

" 'Fraid so," Urias answered.

She couldn't believe her ears. He'd found bear tracks on the edge of the forest. "Won't hogs be mighty tempting for them?" she asked.

" 'Fraid so," he repeated. "I'll stay up most of the night and guard the herd."

She should have been offended that he wasn't thinking about guarding her, but she had to keep reminding herself this wasn't a real marriage. He wasn't a man who loved her. He loved his sister and had done whatever it took to get her free. "I'll keep watch, too."

"One of us should sleep."

"I'll watch the first shift, then wake you. You can watch the second half of the night."

"How is your aim?" he asked.

"Fair. But the shot should be loud enough to hopefully send the bear running."

"Or wake me. I'll load the gun for you, then set up the tent for the night. Are you all set for dinner?"

"Yes. I'll have the quail ready in an hour—possibly a little more."

Urias nodded and left her to her own devices. She knew how to cook, but an open flame scared her. She'd been working overtime, trying not to complain or give Urias cause to send her back home. The truth was, her body ached in places she didn't know she had. She'd always thought of herself as having good stamina, but this walking was pulling muscles in her legs, feet, and back. What she wouldn't give for a warm bath.

She finished plucking the quail and set them on a stick she had braced over the fire, then removed her new shoes. Her feet needed to soak in the stream. Prudence yelped, not realizing just how cold the water had become.

"You all right?" Urias hollered from the edge of the woods.

"Fine," she replied. The stream soothed her aching feet. At first, it felt like needles pricking her, but then her feet were numb to the cold. She stepped out and dried off her feet. What she wouldn't give for a pair of satin slippers. Instead, she put on a pair of wool socks and walked back to the fire. She turned the quail and continued to make the area ready for a meal.

Urias returned with an armful of wood. "This should help keep the bears away. Would you like to practice with my rifle?" he asked. The Kentucky long rifle stood about as tall as Urias.

"If it wouldn't be a bother."

"Be happy to show you. The trick is in the balance of the barrel."

She'd observed Urias for the better part of two days now, and she still couldn't figure out the kind of man he was. He seemed kind but also easily riled. He spoke few words, but when he did, he tried to make pleasant conversation with her. What intrigued her most was his bringing her in on the discussions referring to the purchase of the hogs. No man had ever recognized any points she made regarding finances before.

After dinner, Urias spent a few moments helping her hold and aim the rifle. He showed her how to load and reload it. He even let her do it in front of him, without saying a word. By the time he settled in for the night, she decided he was, overall, a patient man. In her small world, that was a rare treasure.

The various sounds of the night critters kept Prudence

awake. At midnight, she woke up Urias, then crawled into the still warm bedroll. His scent was on the blankets, and Prudence found herself inhaling the teasing fragrance. Sleep came quickly, and Prudence slipped into a deep rest.

The next morning, she and Urias worked better as a team. They each tended to their own chores and found themselves and the five hundred hogs on the road by six. At the end of four days, the rhythm of working together and moving the hogs became smooth. They found themselves at the end of another long day, sitting back and enjoying the stars.

"Prudence, forgive me for asking, but why do you think your father forced us to marry?"

Prudence let out a deep sigh. She'd been expecting this conversation for days. They'd been talking with each other, getting to know one another, but never saying anything deeply personal. "He sees me as an old maid who will never marry."

"Why? You're an attractive woman. You're pleasant company. It doesn't make sense." Urias tossed the remains of his coffee from his cup.

"It's me. I'm the real problem. I like talking finances, and most men feel a woman has no place in business nor the mind to discuss such things. Unfortunately, I've spoken a time or two when I shouldn't have, embarrassing a few men by showing them their errors in calculations."

Urias chuckled. It was the first time she'd heard him laugh. She decided she liked the sound of his laughter and would like to hear more of it.

"My mother—my adopted mother," he corrected, "is very good with figures. In a way, you remind me of her."

Prudence smiled. He'd spoken often about his parents, and the respect he held for them was obvious to anyone who had an ear to hear.

"My folks will help us figure a way out of this marriage."

Shocked, Prudence blinked. She'd foolishly allowed herself to start falling in love with Urias. "We can have it annulled," she said.

"How's that work?"

"I'm not really sure, but I think we simply explain to a judge how we were forced to marry, that we never"—she felt the heat rise on her cheeks—"never had a true marriage, and the judge writes a letter of annulment."

"Would that mean we were never really married?"

"I think so. But I'm not a lawyer, and I've never known anyone who has done it. A few years back, I heard about a marriage the parents had annulled after the kids ran off and married. They were both thirteen at the time. They lied about their ages, so the parents were able to dissolve the marriage."

Something she'd been wrestling with was whether God considered them married. And if He did, were they free to have the marriage annulled? That would be something to discuss with the preacher one day.

"Truthfully, I don't know what is right or wrong here. My folks will help us, I'm sure. But if we got this annulment, what would you do?"

"I'll find a job or something. I couldn't return home. Father would be mortified."

Urias reached over and placed his hand upon hers. "I'll make certain you're cared for."

Prudence changed the subject. "You best get some sleep. Morning is going to come quick." In her heart, she longed to be cherished and cared for. But the man she would like to love her would never get past how they had been forced to be married. "Good night." Prudence walked over to the herd of swine and made herself as comfortable as possible for the first watch. *Lord, I'm so confused.*

❧

Urias's mind was filled with the possibility of an annulment. The four days on the road together had been pleasant enough, but they were not husband and wife. They didn't love one another like his parents—or even his grandparents—loved each other. They weren't even like his biological parents, who'd bickered all the time. *We just. . .are. The only thing holding us together is the mission of procuring Katherine's freedom.*

He had to admit, though, Prudence had not complained once. She worked hard, followed his instructions, and provided security for the much needed rest. He looked out of the tent. Prudence sat, bent over, rubbing her feet, a silhouette painted by a slivered moon. It made no sense to him why any man wouldn't want a wife like Prudence. Any man except him, that is. It was strange. . .in so many ways, she represented the kind of woman he would like to find in a wife. But the reality of how they married could never be blotted out of his mind or hers, he presumed. Why would she want to be bound to a man she'd been forced to marry? It was clear she'd been thinking about an annulment. He hadn't given that idea any thought.

Prudence stood there shaking. Something was wrong. Urias bolted out of the tent. "What's the matter?"

"Nothing," she sniffled.

He lit the lantern and could see she'd been crying. "Prudence, what's the matter?" He trailed the light down her body. Her feet were cracked and bleeding. "You should have said something."

Urias scrambled back to his pack and pulled out some horsetail, then ground the grassy herb into a poultice. He fetched some water from the stream and set the pot on the fire to warm it. "You're riding all day—possibly the next couple of days—on the mule. It's those new boots. I should have known better than insisting on new boots for a journey such as this."

He cradled her feet into his lap and gently washed them. He applied a warm cloth and gently dried them.

"What are you doing?"

"Obviously, I'm washing your feet. Next I'll apply the horsetail poultice and wrap them with clean linen."

As he worked, he felt Prudence relax her muscles and let him apply the healing balm and wrap her feet in a clean, dry cloth. Once done, he took her in his arms and carried her to the tent. "You're going to rest tonight. All night," he insisted. "I'll take care of breakfast. It won't be as tasty as yours, but it'll fill our bellies."

"I'll be all right," she protested.

"Prudence, let me take care of you. It's the least I can do after all you've done. We'll be in Flatlick tomorrow. I have some friends there. I'll treat you to a warm bath. And Mrs. Campbell is a fine cook."

"Campbell? Aren't they the folks who let you hide out in their barn? Isn't that the same place you met your parents?"

Urias smiled. "Good memory. Yes, they are. I was just a naive kid and didn't realize they knew I was sleeping in their barn. Dad pointed out the obvious to me and let me know how it was that I just so happened to find some food around the place." He chuckled at the memory.

"We're through the hollows," he continued. "And tomorrow we'll be traveling on a much larger road." Urias had admired the beauty of the hills, but his appreciation dissipated a little each day with the strenuous march and concentration on the animals. He'd had to help more than one hog out of the briars.

"I should be fine by morning," she argued again.

"Let me take care of you, Prudence. If I have to, I'll simply order you, and you, being my wife. . ."

"Men," she huffed.

"Women," he huffed right back at her. "Look, I appreciate your willingness to help and all the hard work you've done, but your feet are injured. They need to heal, and we have many more days on the road. If we don't take care of them now, they'll get infected and you'll get sick. We can't afford the time for that. I'm merely being practical."

"I see," she acknowledged, her voice strained.

He held the lantern up to get a clear view of her face. "Prudence, I didn't mean to offend you." Urias felt certain this had to be one of those times when men say one thing and women think another. He'd experienced it a time or two watching his parents. They would be trying to explain themselves to one another while neither understood what the other was saying. Eventually they'd work it out, but Mom would tend to get weepy during the process and Dad a bit touchy.

"I'm fine, Urias. I'm just tired and my feet hurt."

"All right." He lowered the flame in the lantern. "Call me if you need anything. I'll make some bandages for your feet in the morning, if they need it."

"You've done enough."

"For being a rich girl, you sure don't like being pampered, do you?"

"Nope. But you're not a poor boy, are you?"

Urias let out a nervous chuckle. "No, I guess not. The MacKenneths own quite a spread, and Dad taught me how to hunt. Before Grandpa hurt himself, Dad used to spend the winter trapping. But the real money came from Mom. I don't know exactly how much it was, but her inheritance seemed substantial. Mom has a real mind for business, quite like yourself, as I mentioned a few days ago. Anyway, she and Dad work out their business affairs together. She's been encouraging me to get into horse breeding, mainly because I like working with horses. But she also sees it as the means for me to make my own way in the world."

"I can't imagine it. My mother doesn't even know what she spends on household expenses. I think Father prefers it that way."

"The MacKenneths are good people."

"They sound it. Kate will like living with them."

"I hope so. Of course, I'll want to build our own house so Katherine has a place of her own as soon as possible."

"She deserves it."

"You best get some rest and let your feet heal. Good night, Prudence."

"Good night, Urias."

She lay down and pulled the blanket over herself. Urias thought back on the image of her cracked and bleeding feet. He should have noticed sooner. *What kind of a husband am I?*

I'm not, he reminded himself.

It would be too easy to forget what happened to force them to marry. How could they possibly make a marriage out of something so wrong?

Urias took up his sentry post. The hogs slept quietly beneath the black sky filled with more stars than a man could count. The moon gave a sliver of a smile. They were getting close. Soon he'd be able to sell the livestock and return to Hazel Green, rescue Katherine, and put an end to this bizarre marriage.

He inhaled the crisp night air and walked closer to the fire. A twig snapped from behind the tent.

six

Prudence savored the memory of Urias's touch. He'd been so gentle, so loving, and yet she meant nothing to him. What would it be like to feel his touch if he truly loved her? She shivered just thinking about it.

"Prudence," Urias whispered. "Stay down; we have some company."

"Who goes there?" Urias bellowed in the darkness.

Prudence stayed in the tent.

"Just passing through." A strange male voice came from the edge of the woods behind the tent. "Saw the fire, wondered if you wanted company tonight!"

"You're welcome to warm yourself by the fire," Urias offered. "Where you from?"

"Hazard. How about yourself?"

"Jamestown," Urias answered.

"Hauling hogs, eh?"

"Yup. What about you?"

"Just making my way over to the ford."

"I have some friends who live around Hazard. Do you happen to know the Fugates?"

"The blue people?"

Blue people? Prudence didn't understand the conversation these men were having.

"Yes," Urias answered.

"Can't say that I know them. Know about 'em, but I don't know them myself. Ain't never had no reason to bother them. How'd you know 'em?"

"My father and I were doing some hunting one year and stumbled into their hollow."

"Folks don't pay them much mind. They stay to themselves."

Prudence's curiosity was up now. But she was under orders to stay put. Yet she wanted to know about these blue people. The test of will began. It had always been hard for her to sit and not speak when she wanted to know something.

"They're good folk. Takes a bit to get used to their color, but after a while you don't seem to notice it."

"Ain't never had an interest. Folks say they're cursed. Personally, I stay away. I'm not saying they're cursed or nothing, but it ain't natural for a man to be blue skinned."

Blue skin? This was too much. She had to know. She opened her mouth, then abruptly closed it. She placed one hand over her mouth to keep from speaking. She thought of all the possible reasons Urias would want her to stay hidden. The stranger might kill her. *That's a good reason.* She removed her hand from her mouth.

Prudence heard the click of a gun.

"Tell your man to step back from the tent," Urias ordered.

Prudence watched the man by the fire raise his hands into the air.

"Tell him," Urias ordered a bit firmer.

"Come on over, Oren."

"With your hands in the air, Oren," Urias added.

Prudence watched with fascination as her husband handled the strangers. *Perhaps they're robbers,* Prudence wondered. She'd never seen a real criminal before.

"Hope you men don't mind sleeping side by side." He ordered the men to lay down beside the fire and tied their hands and feet to one another.

"Sorry to put you through this, boys, but I need to protect my wife."

Prudence's heart fluttered.

"How'd you know he was out there?" the first stranger asked.

"There were two of you when I first called out. But besides that, I could smell ya. Ever heard of soap?"

"We didn't mean anything."

"Let's just say I'm an overprotective husband who can see in the dark."

ॐ

Urias let the guys loose in the morning. Once he exposed their plan, they probably wouldn't have robbed him, but he wasn't taking any chances. He'd leave Prudence with the Campbells and finish hauling the hogs over to the Cumberland Gap without her. With those two out there, he needed to protect her. Mac had trained him well on how to listen and watch the signs of being tracked. All morning, he'd watched to see whether the men had doubled back or continued their way north. Thankfully, they'd continued north.

He'd set Prudence on the mule this morning. She seemed nervous. They didn't talk about what happened last night until they stopped for lunch. Urias heated up some beans and a couple hunks of bacon. "Sorry." He offered her the poor substitute for a meal.

"I should be able to make our dinner this evening." She glanced down at her plate and back up to him. "Urias, who were those men last night?"

"Two lazy men looking for a quick way to earn a dollar."

"Bandits?"

"Not yet. Hopefully, they've learned to stay away from folks traveling on the road."

"How'd you know the other man was in the woods?"

"There were two distinct movements when I called out, but only one man came forward. Which meant the other would circle around and try to sneak up on me. First, they wanted to see how many were in our camp."

"I was terrified."

"I'm sorry about that. We should be traveling with two rifles, one for you, as well. I'm a fair shot, though not as good as my father. He's taught me a lot about traveling in the wilderness. Most of the time you're safe, but the closer you get to the towns, the more you tend to run into bandits."

She took a small bite of her beans.

"It will be all right, Prudence." He laid a reassuring hand on her shoulder. "I'll make certain nothing happens to you."

"You said something strange last night, and the stranger seemed to know what you were talking about. What are blue people?"

Urias chuckled. *If you've never heard about them, it's hard to believe at first,* he reminded himself. "There's a family—the Fugates—in the hills around Hazard. Anyone who lives there knows about them, even if they don't know them. Their skin has a blue tinge to it. Some folks are afraid of them, and the Fugates keep pretty secluded up in their hills. If you're ever in the area, don't mention someone being blue in referring to depression. They'll fear you're cursing them."

"How strange."

"I'll admit it took a bit to get used to seeing them, but they're really fine folks. Nothing different except the skin color. Have you ever been in cold water too long and your lips turn purple?"

"Of course."

"Well, it's something like that. We all have blue in us. If you look at your arms and look at your veins, you see it. For some reason, their skin's just blue."

"Very peculiar."

Urias finished off his beans. "We best get a move on if we're going to make it to the Campbells' by nightfall."

"What about the hogs? Do they have room for all them?"

"Since it's past harvesting time, I don't think there will be a problem with the hogs sleeping in one of the fields."

"A real bed would be nice," Prudence sighed.

He couldn't fault the woman. She'd never lived on the road like this. She'd been treated with a life of luxury. Yet, she never complained. His admiration for her and her strong will increased each day. She'd make a man a fine wife one day. Urias shook off the thought. *No need to go thinkin' like that,* he chided himself, then went straight to work. With everything set to go, he went over to Prudence to carry her over to the mule.

"I feel so useless. Can't I walk?"

"Indulge me. Let's get those feet healed." Urias lifted her. Prudence's unique scent overwhelmed him. "You've got pretty eyes," he blurted out.

Her eyes widened and searched his own. A gentle smile rose on her face. "You and your sister have the same eyes. Not quite the same, actually. Yours seem to have little flecks of gold around them."

He began walking slowly, fearing he would be unsteady on his feet. *How is it that she affects me so?*

Prudence chuckled. "Your ears get red when you're embarrassed. Hasn't anyone told you how beautiful your eyes are?"

"My mom has told me on more than one occasion that my wife. . ." He wouldn't finish that statement. Not to Prudence. This situation was getting awkward, to say the least. He placed her on the mule, forcing himself not to drop her out of sheer embarrassment.

ﱞ

Prudence kept replaying in her mind Urias's touch, his words, his kindness, and his embarrassment. Truthfully, she found herself thinking about him most of the day. She watched how he worked with the animals—how he watched the trail, always alert. He was a true mountain man, or rather one very comfortable in the mountains. There was little more than a path most of this trip down to the Wilderness Road. He took his time herding the pigs through some of the narrow spots.

But mostly her mind kept drifting back to his words: "You've got pretty eyes." A girl could go a week with no food on that compliment. At least this girl could. No one had ever paid her much attention. Father claimed it was because of her constant blabbering about finances. No man would be interested in a woman who spoke on such matters.

But not Urias. He didn't mind. He actually appreciated her business sense. Her heart sank. By forcing this marriage, Father had ruined any chance of her and Urias ever getting to know one another. Urias would never be content to love her. He'd do his duty, but the freedom to love had been stripped away. And, truthfully, she'd never know if he was just doing his duty or truly loved her. More than anything in this world, Prudence wanted to be loved. Her parents loved her in their own way, but they were always trying to force her to be something she wasn't, never appreciating her for what skills came naturally. *Will I ever have my own life?*

"Watch out!" Urias yelled.

Prudence startled from her musings. She jerked the reins. Slippery rocks covered with morning dew sprawled out just down the path.

Urias ran over to her. "Are you all right?"

"Fine. Sorry. I wasn't paying close attention."

"Prudence, I was going to tell you this later, but you're going to have to stay with the Campbells while I finish bringing the hogs."

"I don't want to stay with the Campbells. I want to finish going with you."

"You're not able. By the time I come back, you'll be able to walk again."

"I can walk now," she protested. She didn't mind taking it easy for a day, and her feet were in bad shape, but she could still walk. Painfully, but she still could do it.

"No. Your feet are a mess. I won't be responsible for you injuring yourself. Katherine is my sister and my responsibility," he argued.

"I love your sister and I want to help."

Urias closed his eyes and waited a moment before he spoke. She felt certain he was collecting his thoughts. "Prudence, I know you care for Katherine, and I appreciate all you've done. But, honey, your feet are in serious need of healing."

"Then wait for me. Perhaps we can take a day or two, feed the hogs at the Campbells' farm, then continue on."

"Look, you'll do as I say. You're my wife, and if I say it's going to be this way, then that's it."

Prudence clamped her mouth shut. All the warm feelings she had for Urias had just rolled down the hollow. She would get the annulment and earn her freedom. She would not live under another tyrant.

seven

Urias glanced back at Prudence. By the set of her jaw, he knew she was still angry with him. Ordering Prudence to do anything was not the right course of action. He knew better, but he didn't know what else to say. She was too stubborn for her own good.

The sun was low on the horizon by the time they came up to the Campbells' farm. He ran ahead and knocked on the old farmhouse door. Mrs. Campbell opened it.

"Urias?"

"Yes, ma'am."

"Well, come on in. It's been ages. How are you?"

"Fine, fine. I need a favor. I'm herding some hogs down to the Cumberland Gap, and I was wondering if my wife and I could spend the night."

"Wife? When did you get married?"

Urias felt the heat rise on his cheeks. "Fairly recently."

"Of course, you can stay."

"My wife has injured her feet—from her new boots. I'll bring her in, then take care of the hogs, if that's all right with you."

"Of course. Bring the poor child in. I'll warm some water and get out the salts so she can soak 'em real good."

"Thank you." Urias turned and ran back to Prudence and the hogs. He explained what was going to happen as he led the mule toward the house.

Prudence simply nodded. Apparently she still wasn't ready to speak with him. He lifted her off the mule and carried her to the front door. Mrs. Campbell had him set her on an over-stuffed chair in the living room, and, after a brief introduction, he left the two women and rounded up the hogs. He set them in the fenced-in area to the right of the barn and noticed something was wrong. There was little feed for the winter, and the wood supply wasn't fully stocked. It then occurred to him he hadn't seen Mr. Campbell. He walked behind the barn and found a grave and tombstone. Urias choked down a sob.

He stood there for a moment, then went into the house. "I'm sorry. I didn't know about Mr. Campbell."

Mrs. Campbell's eyes filled with tears. "He died just after planting the west field."

Urias stepped up to Mrs. Campbell and wrapped his arms around her. "I'm so sorry. I'd like to do some chores for you while I'm here."

Mrs. Campbell stepped back and wiped her eyes with her white apron. "I'd appreciate that. I'm going to sell the place and move in with my daughter. She and her husband live in Barbourville. The farm is too much for me, and the boys aren't interested in the place."

In all the years he'd known the Campbells, he'd never seen her sons. He'd heard them talk about their daughter on several occasions. "I'll set you up with enough wood for the winter. It's the least I can do."

"Thank you. Neighbors came around and harvested what there was of the corn. I've gotten rid of most of the livestock, except for a cow, a horse, and the chickens. I can handle chickens just fine."

"Write a list of things you need done. I'll go to the Mercers' place and purchase some grain for the hogs." He turned to Prudence. "If you don't mind, I'd like to stay here for a couple of days and help Mrs. Campbell out."

Prudence's face brightened. "I don't mind."

Didn't think ya would. "Great. I'll be back later. May I borrow your horse, Mrs. Campbell?"

"Of course, son. Do what you need to do."

He wanted to lean over and give Prudence a kiss. Where that thought came from, he didn't want to know. He set his hat upon his head and said, "I'll be back."

Urias headed for the front door. With his hand to the knob, Prudence called, "Urias, aren't you forgetting something?"

She wants a good-bye kiss? He glanced back at Mrs. Campbell. She didn't their marriage was a sham. "What?"

She held up the brown leather purse that held her money.

"Thanks." He winked. He'd completely forgotten about money. He just knew what needed to be done and had only a very short time to do it.

He left the house, readied the horse, and headed for the Mercers' place in less than ten minutes. Mentally, he went through a quick list of what he could do to help Mrs. Campbell out in a day—possibly two. He didn't want to take the time, but Prudence needed it for her feet, and Mrs. Campbell obviously needed some help.

Frank Mercer was more than happy to sell off some feed. He also agreed to send his boys in the morning to give Urias a hand. "They'd been meaning to come by and help Mrs. Campbell anyway," he said apologetically.

Back at the farm, Urias fed the pigs, blending the grain with some water and various edible greens he'd found along the road. After that he went to the woodpile, stacked the split logs, then proceeded to split those already cut. Tomorrow, he'd have to go into the woods and down the standing dead wood.

The clang of the iron triangle that hung on the front porch rang. Urias brushed the sweat off his brow, turned off the lantern, and headed for the house.

"Wash barrel is over there now," Mrs. Campbell directed, pointing to the right rear corner of the house.

"Thank you."

"Don't take too much time. Dinner's getting cold. We've been waiting on you."

"Sorry." Urias snickered as he headed to the barrel. "Women."

❧

Mrs. Campbell's treatment for Prudence's feet had her feeling much better. They weren't as raw as when Urias treated them the night before. Mrs. Campbell also lent her a pair of fur-lined slippers that felt absolutely wonderful. Urias didn't know it yet, but she'd been up walking around and helping Mrs. Campbell prepare dinner.

Urias also didn't know that the room Mrs. Campbell had put them in only had one bed and very little space for Urias to sleep on the floor. Somehow Prudence knew she would have to convince Urias to sleep on the bed. He'd been up the entire night before, worked the hogs hard to come here before nightfall, and he'd been working hard all evening. The man was going to collapse if he didn't get some rest.

She wanted to prepare a hot bath for him but didn't feel she had the right to ask Mrs. Campbell for such a sacrifice. One thing was certain: She'd be leaving with Urias when he left. Prudence didn't want to be glad that Mr. Campbell had passed away, but his passing had allowed her the time she needed to heal and continue with Urias.

The front door opened, and Prudence watched Urias remove his boots before entering. "Evening," he said and smiled.

"Good evening. We've made dinner for you," Prudence offered.

"Come on in and set a spell, son, before you drop. A man can't work that hard and not stop for a rest. Even the Good Book tells us we need to rest."

"Yes, ma'am." Urias stepped into the front room.

"I've set you two up in the upstairs front bedroom. The other rooms are not fit for guests, I'm sorry to say. I've been rummaging through our belongings and deciding what to keep, what to get rid of, what to pass on to others. . . ." Mrs. Campbell sniffed. "It's not an easy task. I hope the two of you never have to go through it."

Prudence didn't know what to say. The woman truly loved her husband and missed him, but she wasn't pining away for him. She was getting on with her life, near as Prudence could tell.

"That'll be fine, thanks. What smells so delicious?"

Mrs. Campbell beamed. "Just something we cooked up."

"We?"

"Your wife helped. She's handy in the kitchen."

"I know but. . ." Urias looked down at her feet.

"They're feeling much better, and with these, it's easy to walk around." Prudence lifted her skirt slightly to give Urias a peek of the slippers.

"They look warm." He scrunched his eyebrows together. "They look familiar." He turned to Mrs. Campbell.

"Good eye, son." Mrs. Campbell led them to the dining room. "They're the pair your father made me several years back."

"Your father made these?"

"Dad is quite handy with animal hides." Urias sat down in the designated chair.

Prudence sat down beside him.

"Shame on you, son. You're as good as your pa. You mustn't keep those hidden talents away from your wife."

Crimson washed over Urias's face.

"Come now. Say the blessing before this dinner is stone cold."

"Yes'm." Urias led them through a brief but meaningful prayer, asking the Lord's blessing on Mrs. Campbell.

"The Mercer boys will be coming over in the morning to help me with the wood. Between the three of us, I'm sure we'll have enough for the winter by the end of the day."

"I can't thank you enough." Mrs. Campbell reached for the casserole dish and offered it to Urias first. He took out a huge helping and passed the dish on to Prudence, who spooned out a much smaller portion.

"You don't each much, child." Mrs. Campbell received the dish from Prudence.

"My stomach hasn't been feeling too well."

"Are you with child?" Mrs. Campbell asked.

Prudence could feel the heat on her face rage as bright as what had appeared on Urias's. "No, I don't believe so."

Urias stared at her and blinked.

Oh no, Lord, I've given Urias the wrong impression. "We haven't been married that long," Prudence amended, trying to motion with her eyebrows that she was saying that for Mrs. Campbell's sake.

⁓

The stew and biscuits stuck in Urias's throat. Had he been forced to marry Prudence because she was with child? Had Hiram Greene seen him as a dupe? Urias's temper rose a notch. He forced the morsel down his throat, closed his eyes, and prayed for grace. If Prudence was with child, that would present another problem. How could he abandon her while she's expecting? And what happened to the father?

He took another forkful of the stew and examined his wife a bit more closely.

"Don't take long," Mrs. Campbell answered.

Prudence's face was beet red now.

Now things were beginning to make sense. Someone had

gotten Prudence pregnant and run out before Hiram Greene knew of his daughter's sin. Which is why he was so upset at their meeting privately in the barn. Would Prudence have tried to seduce him to convince him the child she was carrying was his?

Dear Lord, give me wisdom.

"Forgive me. My daughter and son-in-law are expecting again. It's their fifth. My mind just wanders over to the subject of babies."

Prudence cleared her throat. "It would be nice to have a child one day."

Urias balled a fist under the table, then opened and closed it again and again.

"They are wonderful, but they are a handful," Mrs. Campbell went on.

Had Prudence offered to come on this trip hoping he'd share the bedroll with her? The more he thought of it, the angrier he became.

Urias forced down his meal as fast as he could. He needed to get out of here, away from Prudence, and away from the trap that was squeezing the life out of him. He'd married her for Katherine's sake. She'd married him for herself. All the noble things he'd begun to think and feel about Prudence were all based on lies. She wasn't sacrificing for a friend. She was trying to con him and have him be the father of her child.

Mrs. Campbell finished her ramblings. Urias didn't know what she had said, nor was he in the frame of mind to care. His plate nearly cleaned, he pushed it away. "Wonderful meal, ladies. If you'll forgive me, I have a few more things to do in the barn." He turned to Prudence. "Go on to bed without me."

The chair scraped the floor as he stood up. "Thank you again for your hospitality, Mrs. Campbell."

"Urias, can't it wait until morning?"

Prudence got up and walked over to him. She placed her hand on his forearm and whispered, "It's not what you're thinking."

He wanted to believe her; he really did. But so much had happened in the past week, how could he know for sure? *Time*, he answered himself. Time would certainly reveal if Prudence was with child.

"Urias," Prudence said in full voice, "you haven't slept. You need your rest."

Urias felt the throbbing headache he'd been ignoring for hours. Prudence was right. He needed to sleep.

"Very well. If you'll excuse me, I'll retire for the evening."

Mrs. Campbell smiled. "You two go ahead. I'll take care of the dinner dishes."

Prudence's eyes watered with tears.

Doesn't the woman know how to turn them off?

"I'll show you our room," Prudence said, her words soft and kind, so contrary to the thoughts he'd been thinking about her for the past few minutes.

Silently, he followed her up the stairs. When they entered the room, she turned and shut the door. "You're sleeping on the bed. I won't hear of anything else. I'll sleep on the floor." She wagged her finger at him. "If you say one word of objection, I'll scream, and you'll have some serious explaining to do to Mrs. Campbell."

"What's to explain? You're my wife. My pregnant wife, I might add."

"I am not. Don't you go believing Mrs. Campbell's speculations, Urias O'Leary. I've not"—she pointed to the bed— "with a man, ever, and I'm not about to start tonight. So get your mind out of the pig slop and get to bed before I really say what's on my mind. I'm going downstairs to help Mrs.

Campbell with the dishes. I best find you sound asleep when I return."

Urias let out a strangled chuckle.

"What?"

"You're beautiful when you're angry."

"Ugh." She pushed him backward, and he landed on the bed. She stomped out of the room and down the stairs.

Urias sat up, unbuttoned his shirt, undressed, washed from the basin near the bed, and put on the clean nightshirt Mrs. Campbell provided. He laid back on the bed and thought over the dinner conversation, then the few moments alone with Prudence. *A real marriage with her wouldn't be boring.*

Thump. Glass shattered. A scream bolted Urias out of the bed.

eight

Pain seared her skin. Prudence held her hand over the wound.

"Urias," Mrs. Campbell called out, "come quick!"

"I'm here." Urias stood in the doorway of the kitchen in an oversized nightshirt and bare feet.

"What happened?"

Tears threatened to fall. She wouldn't give in to them. Urias already felt she was slowing him down and wanted to leave her here.

"I don't know."

"It was the strangest thing. We were drying the dishes, and the glass in her hand just shattered," Mrs. Campbell offered.

"Let me see." Urias carefully stepped around the bits of broken glass scattered on the floor.

Prudence looked up at Urias. "I'm sure it's nothing."

"Show me anyway, please."

Mrs. Campbell took a broom from the closet. "Watch your step." She swept the glass from behind Prudence. "Lift her up and carry her out of here," Mrs. Campbell ordered.

He lifted her in his arms. His touch was loving—unlike his words earlier.

"This is getting to be a habit."

"I haven't cut myself before."

"No, I meant the carrying you part."

"Oh." Prudence could feel her face flush.

"I'm sorry," he whispered. "I shouldn't have said those things."

Prudence trembled in his arms. He set her in the same overstuffed chair in the living room. "Let me get a lantern to look at that cut."

Prudence looked down at her arm. Her fingers were lined with blood. *How deep is it?* She fought off the desire to check and kept the pressure on the wound. Her hand was starting to throb from the lack of circulation by her applied pressure. Prudence closed her eyes. The sight of blood didn't help her already uneasy stomach. She always had a fairly weak stomach when it came to certain things.

Urias came in with his hands full. In one hand he had a lantern, in the other, clean cloths and a roll of thin cotton fabric, perfect for dressing wounds. He also carried a bowl with water in the crook of his arm. He placed the lantern on a table and sat down on a stool beside her. "Let me see."

Prudence lifted her hand and looked at the wound for the first time. Her stomach flipped, and a cold sweat swept over her body. The gash was at least three inches long, and she could see bits of fat and muscle. Her stomach rolled again.

"Look away before you pass out on me," Urias ordered. "Please," he said, softening his tone.

She obeyed and looked out the window to the night sky.

"I need to flush the wound before I can bandage it. It should be stitched up. I'll do what I can."

Mrs. Campbell came in. "How is it?"

"Deep, but not too bad. About three inches long."

"I'll get my sewing kit." Mrs. Campbell marched out of the living room.

"I don't have anything to numb the wound. When she starts sewing, it will hurt. I'll hold your arm still for her. Are you all right?"

Prudence bit her lower lip and nodded.

Urias held a clean cloth down on the wound. "You'll do fine. If you can walk on those feet of yours, you should be able to put up with Mrs. Campbell sewing you up."

"Is that supposed to encourage me?" Prudence asked.

"Pay him no never mind. It will hurt like a possum with its tail on fire, but it will heal faster."

Urias got up from the stool and offered it to Mrs. Campbell. He stood between her and Mrs. Campbell and got ready to hold Prudence's arm tight.

Mrs. Campbell positioned both of them, then warned Prudence, "Hold your husband's thigh real tight. When the needle hurts, simply tighten your grasp on Urias's thigh. If he can put up with the pain you're giving him, then you're doing fine."

Prudence wasn't too sure how that would be the case, but she did as she was ordered and reached around Urias's thigh. It was firm and muscular, much the way she imagined it would be. Embarrassed by her own wayward thoughts, she felt grateful that neither Mrs. Campbell nor Urias could see her face.

"I'm going to begin now," Mrs. Campbell said and pushed the needle into Prudence's arm. She bored her fingertips into Urias's leg.

"How many stitches do you think it will take?" Urias asked, his voice strained.

"Far more than I'll put in."

Prudence lessened her grip on Urias. He didn't flinch once the entire time Mrs. Campbell stitched up her wound.

"I'll wrap it up," Urias offered.

"Give it a lot of padding. There will be some more bleeding through the night. Change it first thing in the morning, then you can tighten it a bit more."

"Yes, ma'am. Thank you." Urias resumed his position on the stool.

"Thank you, Mrs. Campbell. I'm sorry about the glass."

"Fiddlesticks, dear. I'm sorry you were injured."

"Mrs. Campbell, if it's all right with you, I'll sleep in another room tonight. Prudence will need the full bed to stretch out her arm."

Mrs. Campbell nodded. "In the middle room, there's a small path to the bed through the crates. Just watch your step."

"Thank you." Urias wrapped the cotton strips around Prudence's arm.

Once she was in the kitchen, Prudence spoke up. "At least neither of us will be on the floor tonight. Thank you."

"Go to bed, Prudence. I'll see you in the morning." Urias walked over to the door, put on his boots, and stepped out. *What have I done now?*

❧

Urias's leg throbbed. He had to get some cold water on it right away. And well water would be the coldest. Ice would be best, but there was none to be found. Even if there was, he wouldn't use it on a wound. *How long are that woman's fingernails, Lord?* He'd almost given in to screaming but noticed Mrs. Campbell was on her last stitch. Outside, he limped to the well. He didn't think she'd broken the skin, but it sure felt like hot pokers stabbing him now. With his luck, he'd be black and blue in the morning.

Urias pumped until a cool stream of water poured into the small bucket at the end of the spigot. He placed the wad of cotton linen he'd brought out with him into the water, then placed it on his throbbing leg.

Before the torture, Prudence's hands had sent a feeling through him that seemed foreign and yet familiar. The contact, for a moment, seemed to almost make him feel. . .feel what? What was the feeling he had experienced? Completeness? But how could there be oneness with a forced marriage? It wasn't a sanctioned marriage. It couldn't be. God wouldn't honor a marriage of this sort.

The Bible story of Esther came into mind. God honored Esther and her marriage to the king, even though he wasn't Jewish. The circumstances of her training to be his wife and of the pagan rituals involved did not honor God, yet God honored Esther and her marriage to the king.

Urias removed the warming cloth and placed it back in the cool bucket.

God may have honored that marriage because He had a greater purpose—the salvation of the Jews from their treatment in that country. Urias's marriage was for a noble purpose—the saving of his sister from her bondage, but. . .could God honor their marriage?

Urias shook the thought off as he placed the cold cloth back on his thigh. When it warmed again, he cooled it again and placed it on his forehead rather than his thigh. His head throbbed from the lack of sleep. He needed to get to bed and recover from the trip, emotional fatigue, and the tremendous burden he'd accepted for the sake of his sister. "Lord, be with Katherine. Keep her safe."

He scanned the heavens. The stars shone in all their glory. "Add Prudence to that request, Lord. The woman tries hard, but she's got to be in pain with those feet and now this wound on her arm. I don't know what to do with her, Father. I do want a wife and children one day, but I'd like to be able to choose who that woman would be. I don't feel right sending her back home to her parents. They don't seem to appreciate her. On the other hand, I don't know what I could do for her. I don't have my own farm to hire her on, but she doesn't seem the sort to work with her hands, anyway."

The past few days' journey floated through his mind. Not once had Prudence complained about the work, the trail, or

her injuries. "She deserves a husband who loves and appreci-
ates her for the way You've gifted her. Father, send her a husband quickly. She needs a husband."

What's she going to do once our marriage is dissolved? he wondered. He removed the cloth from his forehead and combed
his hair back from his face with his fingers. He shook off the
thought and headed back to the house. He needed rest, and
thinking about Prudence would prevent him from sleeping.

ঌ

Urias woke the next morning and went to the barn before the
sun rose over the horizon. He milked the cow, fed the chickens, and took care of a few other odd chores to help Mrs.
Campbell. Her moving in with her daughter seemed the most
logical thing to do. The small farm was too much for a single
person, not to mention an older woman.

The smell and sound of bacon frying in the griddle greeted
him when he walked into the house. Mrs. Campbell stood at
the stove. "Thank you, Urias. It felt wonderful to sleep in this
morning."

"You're welcome."

"How'd you sleep?"

"Fine." Urias placed the bucket of fresh milk next to the
sink.

She smiled. "How's the leg?"

For an old gal, she doesn't miss much. "Sore. . .and shaded with
some interesting colors of purple and blue."

"Sorry. I thought of giving her some whiskey but—"

"Happy to help. The leg will heal."

"Urias, it's none of my business but. . ." She paused to set a
plate of eggs, bacon, and fried potatoes on the table, then
motioned for him to sit down. "How well do you know this
girl?"

His back went stiff. Had she noticed they weren't acting

much like a husband and wife? Or had she seen or heard something from Prudence that concerned her? Urias let out a long, slow breath. "We're still learning about each other," he replied.

❧

Prudence stood on the bottom stair, eavesdropping on Urias and Mrs. Campbell's discussion.

"She doesn't know the first thing about canning and preparing foods for the winter. How's she supposed to handle being a farmer's wife?"

"Guess she'll have to rely on folks like yourself to teach her."

Prudence smiled. Could he be expecting her to become his real wife? Did she want that? Admittedly, the attraction between them was growing. Perhaps that's why it hurt so much to have him thinking she was with child.

Mrs. Campbell chuckled. "You're only going to be here a day or two."

"She's a quick learner. I've been impressed with her on the trail. She's picking up things very quickly."

Mrs. Campbell let out a hearty laugh. "You're doing like your parents, eh?"

Urias chuckled. "Appears that way."

Doing what like his parents? The major problem with eavesdropping was you didn't have the freedom to ask questions when points of interest came up. Prudence stepped down the final step to the floor and walked into the kitchen. "Good morning," she said.

"Morning. How's the arm?" Urias sat at the table with a plate full of eggs, bacon, potatoes, and corn bread. There was enough on his plate to feed two. He sank his fork into his eggs and continued to eat his meal.

"Sore. I haven't looked under the bandage yet."

Mrs. Campbell turned from the stove and placed another

plate with a smaller portion at the place setting next to Urias. "Come, sit down. There's more if you would like some."

"Thank you." Prudence sat down. "This is more than sufficient."

"Would you like me to take care of the bandage?" Urias offered, holding a forkful of eggs halfway between his mouth and the plate.

"If you wouldn't mind. I think I could manage, but it would be awkward."

"Be my pleasure."

Mrs. Campbell set a plate for herself on the table and sat down with them. "Keep it clean and it should heal well."

"I'm concerned about taking you out on the trail for that very reason."

Prudence's heart landed in the pit of her stomach. The fear that had plagued her most of the night had come true. He planned on leaving her with Mrs. Campbell while he finished the trip to the Cumberland Gap.

"Honey, I don't want an infection to set in."

Honey? That's the second time he called me that. Does he actually care for me? Or is this to put up a front for Mrs. Campbell? Urias didn't seem the kind of man that would deliberately deceive folks.

"He's giving good counsel, Prudence. A gal can't stay all that clean on the road. I ain't never hauled no pigs, but when my husband and I were much younger, we made the trip east a few times, bringing sheep and cattle to Virginia. It was an excellent way to earn good money. But the road was dusty."

Prudence sighed. "I suppose you both are right."

Urias reached over and placed his hand upon hers. "I'll stay through tomorrow and set out at dawn."

"Can one man handle all those hogs?" Mrs. Campbell asked.

Urias leaned back in his chair. "I suppose I should hire

someone to come along with me."

"But that will cut the profit." Prudence covered her mouth. The words just slipped out.

Urias smiled. "Right. Why don't we wait and see how your wound is tomorrow night? Then I'll see if one of the Mercer boys can lend a hand."

Prudence lifted her gaze and zeroed in on her husband. Her husband—could her father's arrogance have been a blessing in disguise?

nine

Urias worked hard until sundown. Frank Jr. and Samuel stayed the better part of the day. And Frank mentioned he'd be willing to lend a hand with the hogs if Prudence wasn't ready for travel. Urias knew Prudence didn't want to be left behind, yet what choice did he have? On the other hand, a few days with Mrs. Campbell could be helpful for Prudence to learn more about being a farmer's wife. Not that he was hoping she'd be his "real" wife one day.

As he stacked the wood beside the house that had been split earlier, giving Mrs. Campbell an easier distance to travel in the winter months, the biblical story of Esther popped into his mind once again. Was God trying to say something to him?

The clang of the iron triangle in the front of the house meant it was time for supper. He set the logs on the pile and brushed his clothes down. He needed a good scrubbing, not to mention the state of his clothing.

Scraping his feet on the porch before entering the house, he found Prudence standing at the door waiting for him. "Hi. How was your day?"

"Fine." She held her hands behind her back and had a smile as wide as Cumberland Falls on her face.

"What?" he asked.

"I made you something."

"Oh?" He pulled his boots off and left them by the door.

"Mrs. Campbell would like you to wash up before dinner."

Urias chuckled.

"She put a clean set of clothes for you on the bed. I'm to

bring your dirty clothes down for a good scrubbing."

"They can use it."

"Uh-huh."

Urias fought off the urge to smell his armpits and headed up the stairs, taking them two at a time. He halted halfway up and turned to see Prudence stepping on the bottom step. "What did you make for me?"

"You'll see." She grinned once again.

Urias continued up the stairs and went to the front bedroom. Folded in a neat pile were a clean shirt and a pair of pants.

Prudence leaned on the doorjamb with her hands still behind her back.

"You've got my curiosity up. What are you hiding?"

"You'll see after you give me your dirty clothes."

"Am I to undress in front of you?"

Prudence blushed. "Sorry." She stepped away from the door and waited in the hallway.

Urias closed the door, slipped off his clothes, then reopened it enough to pass them through a small opening. Prudence hesitated, then grabbed the soiled clothes with one hand while keeping her injured arm behind her.

"As much as I want to see my surprise, I think I should wash up and dress first."

Prudence's face beamed hot coal red. Without saying a word, she hurried down the hallway and descended the stairs.

Urias let out a light chuckle, then went to the basin to wash. He looked at the bruises on his leg. They were a deep purple, and the soreness had continued throughout the day. Clean and dried off, he put on undergarments and the shirt, then sat on the bed and wrapped a warm damp towel around the bruised thigh.

"Urias. . ." Prudence opened the door.

He jumped off the bed. The towel slipped to the floor.

"Oh!" Prudence gasped. "Did I do that to you?"

Prudence stared at the bruises on Urias's thigh. "Can I do anything for you? Get you anything?"

Urias cleared his throat. In a whisper, he said, "Prudence, I'm not dressed."

"Oh, right. Sorry." Prudence stumbled out of the bedroom. She assumed he'd be dressed by now. *Why did I come upstairs, anyway?* she wondered.

The bruises on his thigh were the size of silver dollars. The door opened slowly once Urias was dressed. "Come on in."

"I'm so sorry," she apologized.

"It's all right."

"Do they hurt?"

"Huh?"

She pointed to his thigh. "The bruises."

"Not too bad. Now can I see my surprise?"

He was worse than a child at a birthday celebration. "It's not that special, but I had some free time today, and Mrs. Campbell had the yarn so. . ." She handed him the gift.

"A scarf. You made this?"

She didn't know whether to be upset with him for his assumptions about her upbringing again or to take it as the compliment it appeared to be. She decided on the latter. "Yes, I learned to knit from my grandmother."

"It's beautiful." Urias wrapped the scarf around his neck. "And warm, too."

"Thank you. I'm glad you like it."

Prudence then felt that awkward silence that often fell between them when they were alone. Not knowing what to say, she stepped back.

"This is really sweet. Thank you, Prudence. I spoke with Frank Jr. today, and he's willing to lend me a hand with the hogs if you're not up for travel. Speaking of which, how's the arm coming?"

"It's still sensitive, and it's bled a bit, too."

"Would you like me to change the dressing?"

"If you wouldn't mind, I'd appreciate it."

"Sit on the bed and I'll get the supplies," Urias ordered.

Prudence realized she didn't mind his orders—he didn't bark them out like her father. She watched him as he went to the dresser that held the cotton strips of cloth. His red curls seemed masculine on him, quite unlike his sister's, which enhanced her femininity. He turned around.

"What?" he asked.

"It's frivolous really, but you and your sister have the same hair, and yet the curls look feminine on her and not on you."

Urias chuckled. "I'm glad I don't look like a girl."

Prudence blushed. "I didn't mean that."

"No. I know what you mean. I grew my hair out once. Dad wears his rather long. I had to be careful how I brushed mine. If I didn't, you could do me up in a dress and not be sure if I was a boy or a girl. Short hair made more sense. It's easier to care for, and I don't have to worry about it." He approached, carrying the cotton strips for the fresh bandage, and sat down on the bed beside her. "Once I let my little sisters Molly and Sarah play with my hair. They had it all teased up like a bee-hive. If you set a bonnet on my head, I would have looked quite cute."

Prudence giggled. "I'd like to see that."

"Not on your life. Little sisters playing is one thing but. . . well, a man must maintain some level of self-respect."

Without thinking, Prudence reached out and touched his hair. "I don't think you could pass for a woman now."

"Thank you. I tried to grow a mustache, but it's not thick enough yet, and it looked funny—like a fuzzy red worm lying across my lip."

Prudence let out a full laugh now.

"Give me your arm, please."

She reached over to him, and his hands set a flicker of awareness so bold up her arm that she almost pulled it away from his touch. He cut off the knot that held the bandage in place and proceeded to unwind it. With each revolution, her arm tingled as the blood surged through to the wound.

When he reached the pads on top of the cut, he lifted them slowly. In a couple of places, the pad stuck to the wound. "Ouch!" Prudence cried out.

"Sorry. I'll need to dampen those spots. These are probably places Mrs. Campbell could have placed another stitch."

Once all of the bandage was off, she got a good look at the wound. "It's going to be a nasty scar, isn't it?"

"Probably. Depends on how you heal. I scar easily. My dad, not so easily but. . ." His words trailed off.

"But what?"

"Well, Dad's back has these huge scars from when he tried to save his first wife from a bear attack. He was too late."

"I'm so sorry."

"It happened long before I met him."

"You and your family have lived such interesting lives." At the moment, Prudence felt she would love to be a part of Urias's family. He was a kind man, a gentle man, yet she still couldn't figure him out.

"We've traveled a bit more than most farmers. What about you? Did your family ever travel?"

"When I was younger. I remember trips into the city. But for many years now, we've stayed close to home. Father goes off, but he doesn't take the family with him. He says it's business, but I have my doubts." Prudence cut herself off from saying anything further that could incriminate her father.

"Prudence, I know I'm paying more for Katherine's bond than I should. Is your father in financial trouble? Is that why he insisted we marry?"

"No, not that I'm aware." Prudence looked down at her lap and played with the material of her dress. "He forced you to marry me because he doesn't believe any man would want me."

"That's nonsense. You're a beautiful woman."

"Who speaks her thoughts when women should keep silent."

"Look," he said as he lifted her chin with his forefinger, "I know what your father says about women and money, but he doesn't speak for all men. Some of us appreciate a woman with a good head on her shoulders."

Her heart started pounding. She took quick, short breaths. She searched his eyes, those wonderful green eyes. She wanted him to kiss her. Moving ever so slowly, she leaned toward him. And he leaned toward her. He slipped his gaze down to her lips and back to her eyes.

"Prudence, Urias, dinner is ready," Mrs. Campbell hollered from downstairs.

"Be right there," Urias answered. He finished replacing the bandage and took up the soiled strips.

Prudence sat like a boulder on the bed. What had just happened? Were they falling in love? No. . .she'd already fallen. But could Urias feel the same way? *Oh, dear Lord, help us understand what's happening.*

❧

Urias kept his distance after dinner. Out in the barn, he looked for any possible odd job that would keep the separation between him and Prudence. He hoped he could sleep in the spare bed again tonight. Sharing the same room with her right now could prove to be dangerous. What was he thinking earlier?

Fess up, boy. You know you wanted to kiss her and taste those sweet lips. Urias picked up the pitchfork and headed over to the stall.

And that's what bothered him so much. He wanted to kiss her. But what he feared most was that the want would become a need. It was borderline, at best, at the moment. Leaving Prudence with Mrs. Campbell while he finished the trip would probably be best for both of them. They were spending far too much time with one another. He found her to be an attractive and smart lady.

Why had Hiram Greene forced a marriage on both of them? To Urias, it seemed to be more than Hiram Greene's fear that he couldn't marry his daughter off. And this whole business with Katherine's bond being so high after her having worked for two years. . . Well, something wasn't adding up. Urias needed more facts to understand the matter, but he doubted Prudence knew what was going on. She seemed as upset with her father for the forced marriage as he was.

Married to a woman he couldn't touch. It didn't seem right. Everything about this marriage was false. Yet there was something about Prudence that he was drawn to. He recalled her giggle when he'd talked about what his sisters had done to his hair. They were only three and five at the time. It was a fun memory.

Urias pitched the hay from the stall to the wheelbarrow.

"Urias," Mrs. Campbell called from the opened barn door.

"What can I do for you?"

"You can stop taking care of my chores and spend some time with that pretty little wife of yours."

Urias turned away and pitched some more hay. "I will. Prudence understands."

"Does she? I sure don't."

He couldn't explain to Mrs. Campbell. It was bad enough

that she knew that he was married before his parents knew.

Urias placed the pitchfork against the stall. "I'll come in."

"Good. I started some water boiling for a hot bath. I know your wife needs a good soak. She'll need your help washing her hair."

"I can't."

"Why not?"

Urias pulled in a deep draft of air. "Mrs. Campbell, I need to tell you something. When I was a boy, I ran away from my mother because she'd beat me when she was drunk. Apparently, after I left home, my mother started beating my sister, Katherine, in my place. From what Katherine says, Mother sold her into bondage six years ago. She's been working as a servant ever since. It took me five years to find her."

"I'm so sorry, Urias. But what's all this got to do with you not being able to wash Prudence's hair?"

"Prudence's father owns Katherine's bond. Prudence was talking with me about how I could earn some money selling hogs to pay Katherine's debt when her father caught us. And, well, he forced us to get married. He said either that, or I'd go to jail and he'd sell Katherine's bond to someone else."

"What? Is this man a fool?"

"I couldn't wager a guess on that. He's overcharging me for Katherine's bond—of that I'm certain. Even Prudence agrees with me on that. Prudence is my legal wife, but we've not. . ."

"Oh, I see. I'll help Prudence bathe." Mrs. Campbell turned toward the house. "You're welcome to stay in the other room if you wish."

"Thank you. I don't know what this marriage means. Prudence says we can get an annulment, but I want to speak with my parents on the matter first."

"You have my prayers, son."

"Thank you. Prudence is a sweet woman. She's got a good

head on her shoulders, and her parents don't seem to appreciate her."

Mrs. Campbell smiled. "Perhaps the good Lord can take something horrible from this situation and make something beautiful."

Could He? Urias wondered as she left the barn. *Would He?*

Thoughts of Prudence danced through his mind once again—the feel of her soft skin, the gentle fragrance that was her scent. . .a scent so intoxicating it drove him to want to kiss her.

"Argh!" Urias lifted the pitchfork once again.

The sound of a horse's hooves pounding over packed dirt interrupted him in midstride. He turned to see a horse come running up between the house and the barn, its rider hollering, "Is there a Urias O'Leary here?"

ten

Prudence heard the stranger holler and bolted through the front door of Mrs. Campbell's farmhouse.

"How can I help you, sir?" Urias said. It was hard to see him in the moonlight.

"Are you Urias O'Leary?"

"I am. What do you want?"

"I've been trailing you for a few days. Hiram Greene over in Hazel Green said to give you a message."

"What's that?"

Prudence hurried down the steps of the front porch.

"He says you owe him a dowry for his daughter."

"Dowry?" Prudence and Urias said in unison.

"Yup. Says you up and run off with his daughter after you were wed, and since you're taking her from the house, you have to pay him for her."

Prudence could see Urias clearly as he balled his gloved hand into a fist.

"Where are you headed?" Urias asked the stranger.

"Back to Mount Sterling in the morning. Does the owner rent rooms?" he asked, gesturing toward the farmhouse.

Mrs. Campbell placed her hands on Prudence's shoulders. "Don't have any available indoors at the moment. You can spend the night in the barn if you need a roof over your head."

The stranger lifted his hat. "Thank ya, ma'am. I'd appreciate it. The wind's blowin' enough for a storm to come through later this evenin'."

"Very well. That will be two dollars for the night, and I'll have a warm meal for you in ten minutes."

"I appreciate it."

"Urias, would you show the man where he can bunk down for the night?"

"Yes, ma'am."

Mrs. Campbell trailed a hand down Prudence's good arm and tugged. "Come on. We've got another plate to fix." Prudence and Mrs. Campbell headed back into the house to retrieve clean dishes they'd already put away from their dinner.

Who is this stranger? And why would Father say Urias now owes him a dowry?

"Your father must be a strange one," Mrs. Campbell muttered on the way to the kitchen. "Urias just told me about your marriage. Why is he wanting a dowry now?"

"I don't know. I do know some of Father's business dealings in recent days haven't gone so well, but I've never known him to cheat a man. At least not like this. Up a price maybe, but never do something like this. I can't believe it. Mother mentioned something about Urias moving into the house and living there. Can you imagine?"

"No, not at all. Your father has Urias over a barrel, and he knows it. How much were you expecting to earn from the hogs?" Mrs. Campbell questioned.

"With what we owe Thomas Hagins for the hogs, we might have a hundred left after paying the five hundred to Father for Kate's bond."

Mrs. Campbell let out a slow whistle.

Urias came in and stomped his feet at the door. "What is your father trying to pull this time?" he bellowed.

"I don't know."

"Did you and he plan this? How'd that man know where we were?" Urias paced back and forth in the large kitchen.

"Your father didn't even know we were selling the hogs. For all he knows, we're heading to Jamestown to fetch the money from my parents."

Holding down her anger, Prudence said, "I won't even attempt to answer your absurd first question. As for how Father might know where we are, Thomas Hagins could have paid him a visit. He was certainly surprised to find out I was married."

Urias stopped and looked out the rear window. The sun had completely set now, and he stood facing a black canvas.

"Excuse me for interrupting," Mrs. Campbell began, "but I'd say that man in the barn is someone for hire. Perhaps he'd be willing to help you bring the hogs down to the gap. And during your trip, you might find out more about. . .Mr. Greene, is it?"

Prudence nodded.

Urias turned around and faced the women once again. "That idea might have merit, Mrs. Campbell. What do you think, Prudence?"

All the anger she held for Urias instantly dissolved. He was outright asking her opinion. "As much as I don't want to let you go on without me, it might be the best thing. I wonder how much Father paid him to deliver the message."

"Enough to make it worth my while." The stranger stood at the kitchen doorway. He'd come in unannounced and without making a sound.

"Who are you?" Urias asked.

"Sherman Hatfield. I was just passing through town when I heard how Hiram Greene was angrier than a hornet and wanting compensation for you just running off and leaving town with his daughter."

"What about Katherine?" Urias prayed nothing had happened to her since he left.

"Who's Katherine?" Sherman motioned to the table. "May I?"

"Certainly. Have a seat. The food's just about heated up." Mrs. Campbell stirred the meat in the frying pan.

"Thank ya. It's mighty kind of ya, Mrs. Campbell."

"No problem at all. Now, what about Urias's sister, Katherine?"

"Don't know the woman. Can't say."

"She's a bond servant in my father's house. She has long red hair—same color as Urias's," Prudence informed him.

"Oh, I recall seeing her. Frightened little thing. Practically hid in the shadows. Only spoke when spoken to." Sherman locked his gaze on Urias. "She's your sister?"

"Yes." Urias sat down across from him at the table. "Did she appear beaten?"

"No. . . Hey, wait. Are you telling me he beats her?"

"No," Prudence interjected defensively. "My father may be a lot of things, but I've never known him to lift a hand against another."

Sherman gave a nod. "Didn't ya give the man a couple of goats for your wife? Even the poorest of us in the hills pay the wife's family off with something."

"He never asked me to pay a dowry." Urias wasn't about to explain the coerced nature of the wedding.

Mrs. Campbell placed a plate of ham, fried potatoes, and glazed carrots in front of the stranger.

"Thank ya. Smells great."

"You're welcome." Mrs. Campbell sat down at the table. "Set a spell, Prudence."

Sherman Hatfield glanced at each person around the table. "I'm just the messenger. I ain't got nothin' to do with Hiram Greene's personal business."

That might be true, but it was mighty peculiar for a man to

travel this far just to deliver a message. "How long have you been on the road?"

"Three days. You moved those hogs right quick. The trail was easy to follow."

"I wasn't trying to hide out."

"I reckon that be the case. Still, seems odd for you to run off with the man's daughter and not pay the dowry."

"He never stated he wanted one," Urias repeated, defending his actions.

"Urias, I don't think Daddy can charge you a dowry after we're married."

"That is probably true, but you're forgetting he simply won't release Katherine's bond. And he'd have me arrested for running off with his property if I don't pay your dowry." Urias leaned back in his chair. How was the Lord at work in this? He should have gone home straightaway and spoken with his parents. They would have known what to do. At least he hoped they would have. At the moment, he was clueless.

Urias sat straight up and leaned forward toward Sherman. "How'd you happen by Hiram Greene's place?"

"I met up with him in the city. We had some unfinished business. I stopped by to help finish the matter."

"Can you be more specific?" Urias pushed. Something wasn't adding up. No one would travel three or four days out of their way just to give a message that could have been conveyed when Urias arrived to pick up his sister. The more he knew of Hiram Greene's business dealings, the more certain he became that Katherine did not owe Mr. Greene the money he claimed she did.

Sherman scooped the last of his potatoes on his fork. "Mighty fine meal, Mrs. Campbell. Thank you."

He placed two dollars in small change on the table.

❧

Prudence hadn't slept a wink. First she learned that Urias had told Mrs. Campbell their arrangements concerning their wedding. Then the stranger came, giving them a message from Father demanding a dowry. Could life get much worse? *Just when Urias and I are beginning to know one another, this happens.*

Rolling over onto her side, she looked out the window. A light frost had come during the night. Urias needed to get those hogs to the Cumberland Gap. He couldn't wait for her arm to heal, and they couldn't afford any more expenses. How was he going to pay for her dowry? Father had to have some plan or reason to change the debt for Urias, but what? And if he didn't pay, would Father release Kate?

She replayed the same questions over and over again in her mind. Pushing the covers off, she slipped on the bathrobe Mrs. Campbell had lent her and went to Urias's room.

"Urias," she whispered, tapping the door lightly. "Are you awake?"

Hearing no answer, she placed her hand on the brass doorknob and turned it to the right. Prudence stepped into the room and found the narrow pathway to the bed. "Urias," she called again.

As she moved toward the bed, she discovered he wasn't there. "Where is he?" *The barn,* she remembered. *He wakes up before the sun.*

She ran down the stairs and out the front door. "Urias?"

He leaned his red head out the door and smiled. "What woke you up so early this morning?"

She walked to the end of the front porch. She felt the chill of the air on her toes first. "I didn't sleep."

Urias came over to her. "What Sherman said?"

Prudence nodded.

Urias hopped the porch rail and took her in his arms. "I'm

sorry. We'll work this out. Somehow, we'll work this out. I need to take the hogs today. The sooner I deliver them sold, the sooner we can deal with your father."

She shivered in his arms.

He looked down at her feet. "Where are your slippers?"

"I left them in the house. I thought you were in your room."

Urias scooped her off her feet into his arms. "Come on. Let's get you inside."

Prudence wrapped her arms around his neck. Her heart ached over what her father was doing to this sweet man. *He'd make the perfect husband, but he'll never be free to love me, all because of Father.* She buried her head into his shoulder.

"Shh. It's going to be all right. I don't know how, but I know God will see us through. I might have to go home by myself and tell my parents about the situation I got myself into, but I'll be back for you. You can't live with a man like that. There's no telling what he'd do."

"Father's never behaved like this before. I noticed some problems in his financial sheets, but nothing that would warrant cheating a man."

Urias brushed the hair from her face, his touch so gentle, his gaze so consuming.

"You've got beautiful eyes, Prudence."

She felt the blush rise on her cheeks.

"And I love that shade on you."

Prudence gave him a loving swat. She was still in his embrace as he entered the house and carried her up the stairs. *Is he going to. . .* Her eyes widened at the thought.

In her bedroom, he placed her on the bed. He knelt down in front of her and brushed off her feet. "They've healed well. How's the arm?"

"Still hurts." Had she misread the signals? Was he just

being the kind man that he was? Her face brightened another shade.

"Would you like me to change the dressing before I leave?"

"No, thanks. Mrs. Campbell will help me change it."

"All right. Lay down, Prudence." Urias reached out and touched her cheek. "You need to rest, honey. I'll be back as soon as I can."

He tucked her in, then held her hands. "Pray with me, Prudence. Together we'll hear from the Lord about what He wants us to do."

Another jolt of excitement ran through her. This was no longer physical; it was much deeper than that. Urias respected her, believed in her, and wanted to pray with her. He sought her counsel and trusted her enough to pray with him for the answers to their problems.

Tears streamed down her face as she listened to Urias pray, then added her own prayers. He stood up. With his thumb, he gently rubbed away her tears. "God has the answer for us, Prudence. We have to trust Him, because nothing else is making much sense."

"You're right," she admitted.

He kissed the top of her head and slipped out of the room. A peace washed over her. Within minutes, she heard Urias call the hogs and heard them squealing as they exited the fenced-in yard.

Prudence closed her eyes and started to fall asleep.

A loud bang reverberated through the air. Prudence sat straight up.

eleven

Urias held his rifle at the two men who jumped out of the bushes. "You don't want to see how fast I can reload this rifle, do you?"

The two men he and Prudence had met on the trail a couple of days earlier walked out with their hands in the air. "We don't mean no harm."

Urias reloaded the Kentucky long rifle, keeping his gaze fixed on the two men. Perhaps it was time to buy a new firearm that held more than a single shot. "You two didn't learn the first time, huh?"

"We didn't realize it was you," the thinner of the two men mumbled.

"Ain't no never mind to me. I'm still going to bring you in to the sheriff." Urias had the rifle reloaded and ready. "Unless you want to prove to me you can be of more use to society than stealing from it."

"Whatcha got in mind?" the younger man with porcupine-like hair asked.

"If you two help me haul these hogs to the Cumberland Gap, with no stopping to camp—just to let the hogs rest for a spell—I won't press charges. If, however, you try anything, I'll run you in to the closest sheriff faster than you can spit yer tobacca."

They looked at each other and shrugged their shoulders. "Sounds fair."

"Good. Get your packs and let's get a move on." Urias cracked the whip above the hogs' heads to encourage them forward. The two men would test his skills, but they could be a huge blessing. With two additional men pushing at the rear, he could make better time.

"What do we do?" one hollered.

"Cut yourself a willow twig and snap it above their heads and keep walking forward. They'll move."

Urias kept an eye on the road and an eye on his back. He'd made sure the men were not armed. He wasn't letting his guard down for a moment. As they passed the Mercer farm, Frank Jr. met him on the road with a full pack.

"Frank, ask your dad to check on the Campbell farm, and tell him everything's all right."

"Sure." Frank ran up the hill toward his house. Urias caught a glance of the men behind him. "Don't be getting any funny ideas. Frank's dad is a deputy."

Urias heard the men grumble.

Frank Jr. came running back. "Where do you need me?"

"In the rear. Show those two what to do. Watch 'em closely, then send them toward the middle. I'll feel better with you taking up the rear."

"Gotcha." Frank ran to the rear of the herd. He was a couple years younger than Urias. As children, they used to play together.

They kept that pace for four hours, took a break for an hour, and pressed on again. The two would-be robbers actually demonstrated themselves to be quite good with the hogs. In crossing the New River at English Ferry, they swam the hogs across to avoid the ferryboat fee. They continued on that way through the night, and by noon the following day, they had made it to Cumberland County, where Urias sold the swine at $3.50 per hundred pounds, net.

Having more than enough to purchase Katherine's bond and pay Prudence's dowry, Urias gave each man ten dollars with his thanks. Urias learned his two hired hands were brothers, who'd decided that making an honest wage was far more profitable than robbing folks on the road. Frank and Urias spent the night at an inn to let some distance develop between them and the brothers.

The next day, Urias sold the mule and purchased a horse. He and Frank rode the horse back to Flatlick with no evidence of the brothers following behind. They arrived at the Campbell farm, surprised to find more uninvited guests.

"Urias?" Prudence cried and ran to meet him on the road.

"Who's here?" he asked as he slid off the saddle.

"Mrs. Campbell's daughter. We've been packing up her belongings. You bought a horse?"

"Yup. Got a good deal for him. He's no racing horse, but he'll get us through the hollows in more comfort than the mule."

"Didn't Thomas say a mule was better to travel the hollows with?"

"Yes, and I probably should have kept the mule but—it's a long story. I'll tell you after I get to the house."

"All right. It's good to see you. I've missed you. Why'd you shoot your rifle when you left?"

"Again, it has to do with that long story. Have you got a hot meal for a hungry man?"

"Not ready. But I can have one fixed up in no time." Her smile captivated his heart. The push to get the hogs left little time to think of Prudence and their growing attraction. But the ride home with Frank had given him plenty of time to think. Too much time to think. He had the money. He could pay her dowry. But what would happen after that?

"Urias?"

"Huh?" He emerged from his dazed state.

"I really missed you."

Urias nodded. He couldn't speak. His deceitful heart would betray him. A man ought to know better than to give in to a woman who'd been nothing but trouble since the day he'd set eyes on her.

But was it her fault? No, at least not entirely her fault. But if she hadn't come into the barn that second time. . .

And if he hadn't wrapped her in his arms.

"Urias?"

"Huh?"

"I asked how you made out with the sale."

"I got enough to buy Katherine's bond and your dowry. Unless your father upped the price again, I'm going to negotiate low for you."

Prudence's smile faded.

"I didn't mean that the way it sounded. I don't want your father to know how much I earned selling the hogs. He'll ask for more money. I'll offer him three hundred for your dowry, and we'll work from there. How's that sound?"

Prudence cleared her throat.

He'd hurt her again.

"Very wise," she croaked out.

"Prudence, I didn't mean to say you weren't worth more."

"I know."

You have a funny way of showing it, Urias mused. And he found himself constantly feeling hogtied, not knowing what to say or do around this woman. He'd been forced to marry her. He was now attracted to her. But as much as he wanted to, he couldn't trust her, not completely. He wanted to—she'd done nothing to show she was less than trustworthy. Yet still he had his doubts. And those doubts would keep him from taking her into his arms and kissing her. Even though that's exactly what he'd wanted to do when she'd run up to greet him.

Prudence found herself wanting to walk rather than riding double with Urias. Instead, he'd gotten down and led the horse through the narrow spots on the trail. It was well blazed by the hogs. No wonder Sherman Hatfield had found them so easily.

Her time with Mrs. Campbell had been quite an education. She'd learned little things about farming, canning, and planning out the food for the winter. She'd even been taught how to smoke a ham. When Mrs. Campbell's daughter arrived, they spent the entire time making the house ready for Mrs. Campbell's departure and packing up her most precious belongings. Prudence knew she would probably never see Mrs. Campbell again, but the woman had left a mark on her life that would never be erased.

They made camp near a small brook, and Urias set up a privacy area for her to wash. Tonight, she realized, they'd be sharing the tent. There were no more hogs to guard, and, from Urias's tales of the rest of the journey, the would-be robbers were well on their way to making their own legitimate fortune.

The awkward moment came when it was time for them to go to bed for the night. "You can sleep in the tent."

"Urias, that's foolish. We're two grown adults and married. I trust you."

He opened his mouth to speak, then closed it. He didn't trust her. That was their problem. One of their problems.

"You don't trust me, do you?"

He turned away from her.

She walked over to him and placed her hand on his shoulder. "Urias."

He turned, took her in his arms, and captured her lips. Prudence found herself caught up in the emotion and returned the kiss with equal fervor. She wrapped her arms around his neck, and he pulled her closer. Finally, he broke it off.

They stood there for a moment staring at one another. He was breathing hard. Prudence wasn't sure she was breathing at all. She could hear her heart pounding in her ears.

"I'm sorry. That shouldn't have happened. Go to bed, Prudence. Now." Urias walked off to the stream.

She watched for a moment until she saw him pull his shirt off, then turned and ran into the tent. Urias was right. They couldn't spend the night beside one another.

⋘

Prudence woke the next morning, shaking. It was cold, but she doubted the shakes had anything to do with the weather. They'd have to get the annulment as soon as possible. She didn't know how long she could live with this man and be pushed aside time after time.

It was painfully obvious he didn't want to have feelings for her.

"Time to get up," Urias called out. His words were crisp and to the point.

"I'll be right out." She changed into her traveling dress and added another layer of a light wool coat. "It's freezing out here," she said, crawling out of the tent. She stood up and straightened her skirts.

"Warm yourself by the fire while I take down the tent."

"Don't you think we ought to talk about last night?"

"Nope. It was a mistake. It won't happen again."

"Ah." Prudence warmed her back by the fire, holding her palms toward the flames. All night she'd wondered what he would say regarding their passionate kiss. While she could understand him wanting to say it was a mistake, the fact still remained that they were attracted to one another. And with each passing day, she wanted to be Mrs. Urias O'Leary. Yet as they got closer to Hazel Green and her parents' home, she knew Urias wanted nothing more than to rescue his sister and get as far away from her father as possible. She couldn't blame him. Prudence's own contempt for her father grew daily. She had never seen him treat another in business in such a way.

The big question in her mind finally erupted into the open as she hollered, "Urias, when are we going to get the annulment?"

He stopped dead in his tracks and turned around. "We can't until after Katherine is far away from your father. I also will need it in writing that she is sold to me. I won't have that man come after me again for more money."

He was visibly upset.

"Where does that leave me?"

He relaxed his shoulders. "I told you before. I'll take care of you until you can find a husband or a job to support yourself. I've given my word, Prudence. I won't go back on it. I'm not like your father."

She wanted to argue with him about the kiss they had shared. But if Urias was set on his plans to dissolve the marriage and marry her off to the next available man, then she would have to fight her growing attraction to him. Prudence lifted the hem of her skirt and said, "I'll walk first this morning," then proceeded to stomp past him and the horse. *He can load the beast. I'll just continue north.*

❧

Thomas Hagins's farm came into view. *Thank You, Lord, we're almost there.* Prudence and he had barely said a word to each other since last night's kiss. He'd been arguing with himself all night and all day for giving in to such a foolish temptation. He felt a responsibility to her, but what that was, he wasn't sure.

"Mr. O'Leary, Prudence, welcome back. How was your

trip?" Thomas Hagins greeted them as they dismounted the horse. "Where's my mule?"

"I sold him and bought this horse. It was better for traveling with the two of us."

"Them roads through the hollows must be wider than I remember 'em." Thomas scratched his chin.

"Not really—except for the trail the hogs left behind. But that will grow back by next summer." Urias pulled out the money he owed Mr. Hagins, not showing him the rest of his earnings. This trip had made him leery of just about everyone. Generally, he was a trusting soul, but that trust had gotten him in a lot of trouble this trip. First, he ended up with a wife. Second, he had to pay an overpriced bond for his sister. Third, he now had to pay for a wife he hadn't wanted to begin with. He just couldn't risk Mr. Hagins asking for an additional fee, too.

Thomas took the proffered cash. "Was almost hoping you wouldn't return. I could sell that horse of yours for more than what you owed me on those hogs. Ever consider selling him?"

"Nope. He's my stud."

"Fine stock in that one. He's in the barn. I just took him in for the evening."

"Thank you."

"Can I get you anything else? Do you two need a place to stay this evening?" Mr. Hagins offered.

Prudence remained uncommonly quiet.

"No," Urias answered. "Prudence is eager to see her parents." *And I'm eager to get my sister.* The sooner his business in Hazel Green was done, the better Urias would feel. The knot in his stomach had been tightening for the past couple hours on the trail.

"Of course. Well, it's been a pleasure doing business with ya, son." Thomas pumped Urias's hand. "Anytime, anytime."

"I appreciate your trust in me. Thank you."

They said their salutations, and Urias went to the barn to retrieve Bullet. "Hey, boy, how you doing?"

The horse bayed and nuzzled his snout in Urias's chest.

"I missed you, too, boy." Urias saddled the horse and checked his shoes before leaving the barn.

Prudence still sat on the old horse, her back straight and the reins in her hands.

"Ready to go home, Prudence?" he asked.

She nodded her head and nudged the horse forward. Urias trotted Bullet up beside her. He missed their pleasant conversation. The day had been excruciatingly long because of the silence.

"Tonight I'll sleep in your parents' barn."

She turned to him. "Do you think that's wise? Won't my father be expecting us to behave like man and wife?"

"I honestly don't care what your father thinks, one way or the other. He's forced this marriage. He didn't have your best interest in mind. He's up to something. I don't know what it is, but I want to be alert and careful."

"My father isn't a criminal," she defended.

"There are a variety of ways for a man to rob another. Your father's way is more genteel, but it still amounts to cheating a man. And you and I both know he is cheating me."

"Urias, I know things look really bad, but Father's never behaved like this before. I really don't understand why he's doing this."

The sun was setting quickly, and Urias wanted to reach the Greenes' home before dark.

"Prudence, I don't want to argue with you about him. Since he is your father, I'll keep my peace, but I will not relax my guard. I need statements in his writing and to have them witnessed by another. Which of your parents' hired servants would stand by their word that they signed a paper as a witness and won't lie about it later if your father should try something foolish again?"

"You mean which ones can read and write?"

"That, too."

"I can sign. A judge can't say I'm biased, since I'm married to you and he's my father."

"Let me think on that."

"What's there to think on? You can trust me. You know I'm not pleased with Father's actions. . . ."

Urias held up his hand. "It's not that I don't trust you. I don't want to put you in that kind of a position, in opposition to your father. Your relationship with him is strained enough as it is. What are you going to do when you're married and have children? Aren't you going to want your children to know their grandparents?"

"Fine," she huffed.

What did I do this time? Urias wondered.

Twenty minutes later, they arrived at her parents' home. Something seemed odd and out of place. Urias scanned the area. No one moved. Nothing moved. There wasn't even a flicker of light coming from the house.

Prudence jumped off the horse and ran inside, calling for her parents.

Scanning the yard, Urias approached the barn, still on the horse. The family wagon was gone, along with Mr. Greene's horses. Anger burned up Urias's spine. Hiram Greene had run off with his sister.

"Urias!" Prudence screamed.

twelve

Prudence worked at the tight ropes binding her parents. "Urias!" she screamed once again.

"Mother, Daddy, wake up!" How long had they been tied up together?

"Where are you?" Urias called.

"Father's office," she answered. Frantically, she tried to undo the hemp rope knots. They were too tight. "Help!"

Urias ran in. "What happened?" He bent down beside her. "Let me."

With his sharp knife, he cut the handkerchiefs from their mouths first, then proceeded to cut the ropes binding their hands and feet. "Get a couple cool, damp cloths and some water."

"Are they. . . ?" She couldn't bring herself to ask.

"They're alive, but they've been tied up for a while. Hurry."

Prudence ran to the kitchen and dampened a cloth and poured out a glass of water. She ran back to the den and found Urias carrying her mother to the sofa. "Dampen her forehead and face, then start massaging her arms and legs. The blood needs to start pumping."

Prudence did as instructed and watched Urias do the same with her father.

Her mother's eyelids flickered.

"Mom. Mama, can you hear me?"

"Mr. Greene." Urias tried to rouse her father by lightly slapping his face.

Prudence did the same to her mother. "Mama, please."

"They're coming around." Urias shortened the distance and placed a loving hand on her shoulder. "Father," he began to pray, "please bring the Greenes back in good health."

He removed his hand. Her shoulder felt the separation.

"Their wagon and horses are gone from the barn. I'm going to search for Katherine."

Prudence had completely forgotten about Kate and the other servants. "Please do. I'll take care of my parents."

"I'll return as soon as I can. Where do you suggest I look first?"

"Her room. It's at the end of the hall upstairs."

He ran out of the room. She couldn't blame him. *Where is Kate? And the other servants?* She continued to rub her mother's hands and feet, alternating every few minutes and doing the same to her father. *What happened here? Robbers?* She'd never heard of such a thing in the area. But someone had taken her parents' wagon and horses. And someone had left them tied together to aid in their escape. But who? And why?

Prudence pondered the many questions in her mind over and over again. Her father wasn't in the kind of business that brought unsavory characters into the area. What had happened?

She'd been working on her parents for what seemed to be an eternity, yet only three minutes had passed. Urias hadn't returned. She didn't like not having him beside her. He brought comfort and peace into her life just by being there. *Oh, Daddy, how could you have ruined my only real chance of happiness by forcing Urias and me to marry?* Her unspoken thoughts had plagued her constantly each day she spent as Urias's wife.

Her father moaned.

Thank You, Lord! "Urias! Father is coming to," she called out. She wasn't sure if he could hear her, but if he was within earshot, he would want to know. Wouldn't he?

"Prudence, get another cloth for Katherine." Urias carried his sister in. "There are a couple of others in the same shape. I'll bring them in here." He placed Katherine on the floor and scurried out of the room.

Prudence placed the cloth from her mother's forehead onto Kate's, then ran to the kitchen, pulled a couple of towels out of the cabinet, and pumped a bowl and pitcher full of water. Father always had a few glasses in his office.

Back in her father's den, she found Urias had deposited Franni, the cook, and Henry, who'd been working for her parents for as long as she could remember, on the floor near Kate.

"Prudence," her father's hoarse voice called out.

⁂

Urias sat in amazement listening to Hiram Greene tell his tale of what happened. Something wasn't adding up, and, by the look on old Henry's face, he knew it, too. When the hour grew late and the women had settled in for the night, Urias stopped Hiram in midstream. "The women are gone. Tell the truth, Mr. Greene. This wasn't your average robbery," Urias challenged.

"The boy ain't so dumb, is he?" Henry spoke up for the first time.

"Hold your tongue, Henry," Hiram barked.

"Look, as best I can tell, you owe someone a large amount of money. You've asked for more money than my sister's bond is really worth." Urias held up his hand to stop Hiram Greene from defending himself. "I'm going to pay you what you asked for, but don't take me for a fool. You also sent word that you wanted a dowry for your daughter. Now, that says plain and simple you need money and you need it fast. Am I correct?"

Hiram fell back into his chair.

"I'll be leaving now. Thank ya again for savin' us, Mr. O'Leary. Don't knows how I could ever repay it." Henry extended his ashen hand, and Urias shook it.

Hiram Greene kept his head bent down. Urias leaned on the desk, hovering toward Hiram Greene. "Now, are you going to be straight with me?"

Hiram looked up with bloodshot eyes. "It's just a temporary setback. I gambled on the horse race and lost a lot of money to a man who apparently takes his gambling wagers seriously."

"How much do you owe?" Urias pushed away from the desk and sat down across from his father-in-law. It seemed impossible to believe that he was now related to this man. But family is family, and even if it was only on a temporary basis, there were ways a man should treat another even if the other didn't treat you the same.

"Fifteen hundred—if Sawyer Bishop doesn't deduct the value of the items he removed from the house."

"And where can I find him?" Urias stood up and grabbed his coat.

"What are you planning to do?"

"I'll offer him a compromise on your debt. I can't pay it all, but I can come pretty close. That should appease him long enough for you to raise the additional $250."

"I don't know when I can pay you back."

Urias placed his hands on his hips. "Let me make one thing perfectly clear. I'm not giving you a loan, nor am I paying a dowry for your daughter. You did not ask for one when we were forced to be married, thus it is not required of me to pay you one. However, with that being said, you are family, and I will help you this one time. I will not expect to hear from you again concerning any financial arrangements between us. I will pay what is due for my sister's debt. The additional funds are a gift."

All sorts of admonitions and exhortations begged to come out of Urias, but he held his peace. Only God could convict a man like Hiram Greene. No amount of human reasoning would get through to him. He looked at life through the narrow focus of his own needs and didn't notice anyone or anything around him unless it served his own personal gain.

"Before I leave, I want my sister's release from your bondage."

Hiram dipped a pen into a small jar of ink, tapped it on the rim, then wrote a simple note. He blew it dry and handed it to Urias.

"Thank you."

"You can find Sawyer Bishop a couple towns over in Salyersville."

"I'll return tomorrow evening." Urias slipped out of the office with the paper in his pocket.

Prudence met him in the hallway with tears in her eyes. "You don't need to do this."

"For your parents' sake, I must. Now, you and Katherine get ready for our trip to Jamestown. We'll leave day after next at first light."

"What about the annulment?"

Urias's back stiffened. They had agreed on an annulment. But that kiss still blazed in his memory. She was right. An annulment was best. "We'll take care of that in Jamestown, after I get you out of harm's way."

He turned to leave.

"Urias."

She stood there shaking. He wanted to take her in his arms and chase away her worries and fears. "It'll be all right, Prudence. Pray for safe travel."

"I already began."

He chuckled. "Your father doesn't know about that closet?"

Prudence smiled.

"What closet?" Hiram Greene asked.

ᓚ

If it hadn't been for her father's contrite spirit after coming so close to death, Prudence was certain she'd be unable to sit for a week once he'd heard how she'd eavesdropped on his business meetings.

The next evening, she and Kate were packing their bags in Prudence's room. For the first time, Kate hadn't had to work to serve the family. Prudence wanted to treat her as an equal. Admittedly, she had treated her as a servant even though she'd been a close friend. "Kate, the weather is getting colder. Wear two dresses. That will give us another layer and an additional dress for when we arrive in Jamestown. Without a wagon, we can't bring much."

"Tell me. What's my brother like?" Kate pleaded.

"He's a kindhearted man. And I've never met anyone so aware of what's happening around him. The night we ran into a couple of robbers—"

"Robbers?"

"Yes. Oh, Kate, I was never so scared. But Urias stayed in complete control. I felt so calm and peaceful around him. I've never felt that before, even with my own father." Prudence stopped herself from revealing her heart. She and Urias would be filing for an annulment as soon as possible. No need for Kate to know the truth. "You'll be proud he's your brother."

"It's all so strange. I know he's my brother, but my brother was this small, gangly boy that left home years ago."

Prudence held off the images floating in her mind of just how handsome and rugged Urias was. Her heart actually quickened its pace when she saw him. "It must be. But he's a caring man. He stayed an extra day in Flatlick just to help a widowed friend."

"Is he a good husband?"

How do I answer that one? Truthfully, she decided. "Given the right situation, I think he'll make someone an excellent husband." Prudence lowered her voice. "Urias and I will get an annulment as soon as possible. I can't trap him in a marriage that isn't a real marriage. He deserves a wife that will love him for the man he is."

Kate stopped packing and put her hands on her hips. "I don't understand. Why would he be paying your father's debt?"

"Neither do I. He's a man of honor and principles; that's for certain. But I don't begin to understand what goes on in his mind."

"He sounds a bit like our father, from what I can remember about him. Pa knew our mother was drinking too much. And he tried to keep her away from the drink. Once he died, she had no one to stop her, and she got bad. Real bad. She never beat me as badly as she beat Urias, though."

Prudence took in a deep breath. "Father hasn't been the best man to live around, but he's never laid a hand on either myself or my brother. I can't imagine what it was like for you or Urias."

"You don't want to." Kate placed her dress in the carpetbag. "What about these?" She held up the silver hairbrush and mirror that had been handed down from Prudence's grandmother.

"I'll wrap the mirror in one of my dresses. I can't take many personal items, but that's small enough and important enough to take with me. Perhaps in time I can return and pack some more of my things."

"Did Urias speak of his home? What's it like?"

"He lives with his adopted parents. But he mentioned he was going to build his own house soon. He said it was a large farmhouse. He didn't go into details of how many rooms and such." Prudence wondered if there truly would be room for her and Kate in the house. She also prayed for the hundredth time for Urias's safety.

"When do you expect him back from his errand?"

"I don't know. He seemed to think he'd be back in time for us to depart as soon as the sun rose over the horizon tomorrow. I hope he arrives soon."

Kate cocked her head to the right and scrutinized Prudence. "You love him, don't you?"

Feeling the blush rise in her cheeks, she turned back to her packing. "I'm simply concerned for him, is all."

Kate chuckled. "You can try to deceive me if you wish, but I see that light in your eyes every time you speak of him."

"I don't know if I love him. I do care. But love takes time for a man and woman to discover. How can someone love a woman he was forced to marry? It doesn't seem right."

"I guess you're right." Kate went back to her packing. "I ain't never been in love. Ain't likely to happen, either."

"You can't say that, Kate. You never know."

"Perhaps."

Prudence saw that far-off look in Kate's green eyes. Prudence vowed never to push Kate to tell her about her past. The bits and pieces she had shared were enough to know it had been a horrible time since she was sold into bondage by her mother. Mrs. Campbell had shared with her some of the things that could happen to servants and slaves by their owners. She prayed Kate could move beyond her past and feel the peace Prudence felt around Urias.

"God may just surprise you yet."

"You know I don't give no never mind to Him. He ain't helped me a day in my life." The bitterness of the past tinged Kate's voice.

Prudence reached over and lovingly placed her hand on

Kate's. "I know you have a hard time believing in God, but He's real. And isn't it likely that Urias finally finding you before you were sold again was God's answer to Urias's prayers?"

Kate softened. "Maybe. But I ain't giving God credit. Urias found me."

Prudence knew Urias to be a godly man. How would he deal with his sister's unbelief? Would the MacKenneths accept Kate in their home, knowing she didn't believe in God?

Prudence resolved that if the MacKenneths wouldn't allow her to live there, she'd have Kate live with her. Together they would be able to provide for themselves. She hoped.

Prudence heard the sounds of approaching hooves. She glanced out the window. A solitary rider approached the house. *Urias*. Her heart skipped a beat. Kate was right. She did love this man.

thirteen

Urias drove the wagon back to Hiram Greene's estate. He'd been battling with the Lord and his anger the entire trip. He never would have guessed the cost would be so great. It was one thing to give a man money—quite another to give him your future. *And for what? A man who hogtied me into marrying his daughter?*

"Yah." He snapped the reins and encouraged the horses forward. Bullet had been his future, his farm—his stock. Now he'd have to wait another season or two to get another stud like Bullet. Thankfully, he still had the mare and stallion back on the farm. But you never knew if you'd end up with a male or female or one with lines as excellent as Bullet's.

"Lord, I can't begin to understand why I had to sacrifice the horse for Hiram Greene. But Sawyer Bishop wouldn't hear of any other arrangement once he caught sight of Bullet. I still have a substantial amount of money after exchanging Bullet for part of the debt, but it's a cold compromise." Urias took in a deep breath and watched the white vapor rise from his mouth. "I'm sorry, Lord. I'm just having a hard time accepting how much this is costing me. First, I get tied down with a wife I don't want. Then, I get involved with another man's troubles. When is it going to end?"

The stars flickered in the black velvet sky. There was little Urias could do. He could have left Hiram Greene to the repercussions of his own making, living out his own bad decisions. But that wouldn't be fair to Prudence. Not that she would have known. Well, besides the fact that he and Prudence had

113

come upon her parents near death's door. How long would they have survived in those chairs?

The memory of Kate's pale face and bluish hands still made him tremble. To do business with a man who could do that to others seemed wrong, terribly wrong. And yet there had been little choice. If he were to live with himself, he had only one option and that was to give up Bullet and his future. He was beginning to wonder if he'd be tied down to Prudence the rest of his life, as well.

He'd never know the kind of love his parents knew. He was destined to live out a life of servitude for the sake of others. "How unfair is that, Lord?" he called out to the heavens.

A single rider passed him on the road to Hiram Greene's estate. "Nice night," the stranger called out.

"Bit chilly," Urias replied.

"Grows hair on the chest." The stranger chuckled and headed off.

Five minutes later, Urias found himself in Hiram Greene's barn, unfastening the horses and settling them with some fresh water and oats.

"Urias?" Prudence called as she ran into the barn. "You got Father's carriage and horses back."

"Yup," he mumbled.

"Are you all right?"

"Fine. Fine."

"I saved some dinner for you. Come back to the kitchen and I'll heat it up." She flitted out of the barn as swiftly as she came in.

He wasn't in the mood to play husband and wife. She could try all she wanted, but she really wasn't his wife.

If she didn't care, would she have bothered with your dinner? he challenged his own wayward thoughts.

"Urias," another feminine voice gently called. Katherine

came into the barn a bit more timid than the last time he'd seen her.

"Katherine, you're looking better."

"Thanks to you and Prudence. She says you are going to build your own house when you return to your family's farm. Is this true?"

I'd been planning on it. "Not until spring. More than likely it will take me a year or two."

"If you don't mind me asking, where will I be staying?"

"I'll set you up in my room. I'll make a spot for myself in the barn. You and Prudence can share my room. It's a busy household. I'll enjoy the peace."

"What do you mean?"

"Don't get me wrong, I love my younger brother and sisters, but they can be a handful. Little Nash gave me this for the trip." Urias reached in and handed Katherine the arrowhead. "It's in case I run out of bullets and run into a bear. Of course, the poor boy doesn't know I wouldn't have time to fashion a bow and arrow first, but it's the thought that matters. You'll like him, Katherine."

Katherine hunched her shoulders. "I'm nervous about going there, Urias. I won't fit in."

"You'll fit in just fine. Remember, these folks have been praying for you and your safety for years."

Katherine opened her mouth to speak, but closed it instead. *How peculiar,* Urias thought. It's the second time he'd referred to God and had a negative response from her. Urias pinched the bridge of his nose. His sister had been through a lot. She didn't say anything about it, but she didn't have to. The way she walked, the way she held her shoulders, her head—everything pointed to a life of abuse and little encouragement. "It'll be all right, Katherine. Trust me."

"I'll help Prudence warm up your dinner." And that was

that. She was gone as quietly as she arrived. Only this time, Urias knew what she was thinking. Trust.

❦

Prudence placed the cast-iron frying pan on the woodstove in the kitchen. She took off the kettle of hot water and poured it over some coffee grains.

Kate stepped into the kitchen and removed her shawl. "Did you see Urias's horse in the barn?"

Prudence thought for a bit. "No, I don't think I saw Bullet. You don't suppose. . ." Her words trailed off.

"I don't know horses, but the way your father was carrying on about Urias's horse, I figure he was worth something."

"Yes, he was. Urias was planning on using that horse to start his farm for breeding horses."

Kate went to the cupboard and pulled down a plate for Urias. "Do you think he had to trade his horse for your father's debt?"

The back door creaked open.

"Yes, but we won't speak another word on the matter, is that clear?" Urias said as he scrutinized Kate and Prudence.

Prudence nodded and turned away. *Father not only cost Urias and me the chance of ever having a real relationship, he's now cost Urias his future.* Prudence took the wooden spoon and stirred the beef and gravy stew.

"Smells great." Urias gave a mock smile when she looked up.

Kate put her hands to her hips and said, "If we be of a mind to question you, you ought to be of a mind to tell us. What happened?"

Urias pushed up his sleeves and dipped his hands into the washbowl by the back door.

"Let's just say there was little negotiating with Mr. Bishop. I had to pay in full. He wouldn't accept a partial payment, no matter how large it was. Now, I don't wish to discuss the matter again. I did what needed to be done, and that is all."

Her stomach quivered, and Prudence fought the shakes at hearing the great sacrifices Urias continued to make for her and her family. He didn't need to. He just did. She'd never met a man like him. But she also felt terribly guilty for the actions of her father, for the condition of his financial affairs, and for the abuse Urias had taken out of concern for his sister. Her disappointment in her father rose once again. "You should tell Father. Perhaps he'll pay you back."

"As I said, ladies, I will not discuss this further."

Prudence's back stiffened at Urias's firm tone. He'd seldom been that sharp with her on the trail. She glanced over to Kate and noticed her shoulders squared.

"Forgive me." Urias sat down at the kitchen table. "It's been a long day, and I've had little sleep. If you'll be so kind as to serve me up a plate of that wonderful stew, I'll be more fit for company."

Prudence filled the plate. Kate cut him a thick slice of bread and placed it in front of him.

"Thank you, ladies. This is a fine meal, indeed. How is the packing coming?"

"We're just about ready," Prudence offered. "Without Bullet, perhaps we should consider bringing less."

Urias scooped a forkful of his supper, then put his fork back down on his plate. "Please sit down and join me." He reached out both of his hands. "Pray with me."

They joined hands, and Urias led them through a brief prayer, thanking the Lord for His many blessings and asking for safety on the trip home.

"How long will the journey last?" Kate asked.

"By horseback, three days—possibly a piece of a fourth. Walking it will take several days more. However, I have a mind to speak with Thomas Hagins again and see if I might be able to purchase another horse and a small wagon. Because Bullet was so valuable, I still have some money."

Prudence looked over to her husband. What was he thinking? Obviously, he was upset to lose Bullet, but how could he be upset one minute and calm the next? She looked over to Kate, who seemed just as puzzled about Urias's behavior.

"What's all the tongue wagging going on in here?"

Prudence watched her father walk into the room.

"Mr. O'Leary, you've returned."

Urias wiped his mouth on the cloth napkin. "Yes, sir. Your debt is paid in full."

Prudence watched the silent communication that flowed between Urias and her father. Something else, or some greater sum of money, was owed. Her father's face brightened to a deep crimson shade. His shoulders slumped, and he looked down at the floor. "Thank you. I'll pay you back."

"That won't be necessary." Urias sopped up the last of his stew from his plate with the remaining corner of his bread. "We'll be leaving in the morning." Urias stood up from the table. "Thank you for the dinner, Prudence, Katherine. I'll see you in the morning." He placed his hat upon his head and slipped out the back door.

Prudence turned and looked to her father for a possible answer to Urias's bizarre behavior. Her father's face reflected a similar guarded expression. He excused himself and silently departed the room.

Kate looked at Prudence. "What is going on?"

fourteen

Hiram Greene had a lot to answer for, but Urias felt convinced he wasn't the man to address him on the matter. It was all the years of listening to Dad telling him to respect his elders, Urias figured. It didn't make much sense with a man like Hiram Greene—he'd been fooling his family and neighbors for years. Urias now knew his secret and, he prayed, Hiram's shame might keep him from making the same mistake twice. One thing was certain: Urias had never been put in such an awkward position before. Hiram's life and the lives of his family would have been in jeopardy if Urias hadn't paid off Mr. Greene's gambling debts.

Gambling was one of the hesitations Urias had about raising horses. Horse racing was becoming a statewide interest for folks in Kentucky. And folks were willing to pay well for good horse stock. Urias enjoyed horses, and Bullet had been his pride and joy. He'd bred him to be a fast horse with strong lines, and he was. Now someone else would be earning the money from breeding Bullet.

Farmers had need of a horse that could haul the plows and work hard to earn their keep. They didn't have to be fast, but they did have to be strong and steady. Unfortunately, the average farmer was unable to pay higher prices for a good racehorse. Urias had heard that the army was always on the lookout for good, strong stock. But profit would be slower in coming, and it would take more time to earn the funds needed to build his own house. That was something he'd been dreaming of for a long time, but something even more pressing, now that he'd found Katherine.

Bullet would have been the stud he would rely on to develop his horse farm. But Bullet was gone, and so were the dreams and plans he had for the future. *How am I going to provide for Katherine and Prudence, Lord?*

"Urias?" Prudence called from the barn door. He'd slept in the barn last night. Hiram Greene hadn't even offered him a bed.

"Unbelievable," Urias muttered, then said aloud, "I have our horse just about ready. Are you and Katherine all set?"

"Yes, but breakfast is ready. We've been cooking for an hour. Mother had us make some provisions for the road."

Prudence stepped closer toward him. "Urias?"

"Hmm?" he mumbled while cinching the saddle.

"Mother wants to know why you didn't spend the night with me."

Urias couldn't believe Prudence could be so open with him. She truly deserved better parents. "What did you say?"

"I told her we don't see ourselves as truly married."

"What did she say?" Urias asked, then turned to face Prudence. Her beauty made him question more than once why they hadn't acted on being man and wife.

"She suggested I stay home and let you go your way with your sister."

He didn't expect to hear that. Then again, Prudence and her family were full of constant surprises. Urias cleared his throat. "Is that what you would like?"

"I don't know." Prudence sat down on a sawhorse. "I've been wanting out of my parents' home for a very long time, yet we aren't truly man and wife. I can't live like this, either. But you've given so much to my family. I can't begin to understand why you needed to give Mr. Bishop Bullet for my father's debt, but I trust your word on it."

"Prudence, you and I both know this marriage is a sham. We married to secure Katherine's freedom. If you would like to stay in your parents' home, I will not stop you. I'll sign whatever papers you wish to dissolve our marriage."

Tears welled in her eyes. Urias wanted to reach out and hold her. He kept his hands in place.

"I want a real husband, Urias. But I need a man who can respect me and what I think on matters. All the men in this area, the marrying ones, are not interested in a woman like me. Are there others like you and your family in Jamestown?"

Urias felt his gut wrench. The idea—the thought of another man holding Prudence. . . He shook the thought away. She didn't belong to him. He had no rights to this woman. "I suppose there are some. I never gave it much thought."

Prudence sighed. "My family has been enough of a burden to you, Urias. I'll stay."

The tears that had threatened to fall now ran silvery tracks down her cheeks. She stood up and headed back out the door. "Come in and have a warm breakfast before you and Kate leave," she called over her shoulder.

Stunned, Urias stood there gazing at the open door with the sun rising over the mountain. Then it hit him. He'd been afraid all along that she, as well as her parents, had cooked up this marriage. Now he was certain. They had all used him. They used him to pay off their personal debts. *Well, she might think she's free. . . .*

Urias stomped out of the barn and toward the kitchen.

☙

Urias marched to the table and sat down without washing up first. Prudence thought to suggest it, but there was something in his rigid movements that she recognized. He was upset. *Does that mean he wants me, Lord?* She fought off the foolish thought and asked, "How would you like your eggs?"

"Fried." He placed his napkin in his lap. "Prudence, I've given the matter some thought. You'll come with me and work off your father's debt."

"What?" Anger burned in her heart. Hot tears formed in her eyes. "Fine. Anything you say."

"You can be my bond servant," he said.

Prudence took quick, short breaths. She was to be her husband's slave? The man she loved wanted to treat her like property? Her hands shook as she dropped the eggs in the frying pan. They sizzled against the hot iron. "Fine. But if you don't mind, please don't tell my parents."

Urias coughed, then gave a slight nod.

Prudence finished cooking his eggs and placed them on the plate in front of him. She discarded the pan and left him to his meal. After all, a servant wasn't allowed to eat with the family. In her wildest dreams, she never would have thought Urias to be so cruel. If being a servant was what it would take to help her parents, then she'd be the best servant she could. Truthfully, she'd have to rely on Kate instructing her in how to do most of the tasks.

She ran up the stairs and collapsed on her bed. A couple minutes ago, he'd been so reasonable. Not that she didn't want to be with Urias—she ached to be a real wife to him. But now she couldn't imagine it. Perhaps it was a good thing they weren't really husband and wife.

"Prudence?" Kate called. "What's the matter?"

"Nothing." Prudence wiped her eyes. "Urias is eating. We'll be leaving soon."

"I'm all ready. I'm scared," Kate confessed.

Me, too. "It'll be all right. He loves you." *Unlike me.* Prudence knew self-pity would get her nowhere. She would settle up with Urias just how much she owed and how long it would take for her to work off her bondage. She would not allow him to treat her like others had treated his sister. *Did he forget that I gave up my life for Kate, too, Lord?*

Prudence followed Kate down the hall and down the stairway to the kitchen. It struck her odd knowing that Kate was once her servant, following orders, and now she would be Kate's servant. *Father, give me strength. Help me to not displease Urias,* Prudence silently prayed.

&

The eggs and sausage sat in the pit of Urias's stomach. He'd gone too far with Prudence. He never should have insisted that she be his bond servant. Her working off her father's debt would have been far more than enough of a sacrifice. But he'd been angry, and when he was angry, he could get himself into a heap of trouble.

Scouting ahead, he checked the trail before the women passed. Being alert would take all of his concentration. Sleep had eluded him last night, and after the two days of hard travel, he should not have insisted they be on the road so early this morning.

Hiram Greene had fumbled over his words of thanks when Urias and the ladies departed. Urias even thought he saw a tear in the man's eye when he gave his daughter a hug and a kiss good-bye, confirming Urias's darkest thoughts of the plot the parents and Prudence must have put together. It was Prudence who sought him out and suggested they run the hogs to the Cumberland Gap. It was Prudence whose bold presence in the barn caused Hiram to be angry and force a marriage upon them.

It took effort to lift his feet off the ground and place them in front of him. If walking was this difficult, how was he ever going to get these women to Jamestown? He glanced back at the women. They seemed to be talking about him. The way Katherine kept looking at him, the way Prudence kept avoiding looking at him. . . She must have told Katherine he'd made her his bond servant. Urias groaned. This would be the longest trip he'd ever been on.

He scanned the area in front of him and pushed himself to keep walking. Running might be better. Even his parents would not be happy to hear what he'd done to Prudence. Admittedly, he wasn't too proud of himself, either. On the other hand, everything seemed to add up that Hiram and Prudence had conspired against him. He was an easy mark. Hiram held Katherine's bond and realized Urias would have done anything to gain his sister's freedom, including paying higher than normal fees and bringing those hogs to the Cumberland Gap. A smile swept across his face.

He had enjoyed that trip with Prudence. She'd been more than just a good traveling companion. The memory of the kiss they shared stabbed his conscience. She felt so wonderful in his arms. The kiss, so warm and inviting.

Urias shook off the memory. *The devil comes in all forms,* he reminded himself.

The only real question was: How soon could he have this marriage annulled?

&

"I'm scared, Pru. If he can do to you what others did to me. . . I'll be surprised if he doesn't treat me like a servant, too."

"Something happened when he went to pay Father's debt." Prudence gnawed her lower lip. "I could have had the marriage annulled immediately, and he was free to leave with you."

"Why is he making you work for your father's debt?" Kate tossed her head from side to side.

"I don't know." *Why did Father make Urias pay for Kate's debt?* Maybe she truly didn't understand business matters. As her father suggested time and time again, it's a man's world.

Prudence was afraid to speak her fears. How was it that the

man she started to understand on the trail was not the same man on this new trail? It didn't make sense. But then again, nothing had made sense since Urias O'Leary came into her world. And sharing her fears with Kate, who seemed to live in constant fear, didn't seem fair to her.

"Kate, we'll have to trust the Lord for our protection."

"Humph." Kate snickered. "Ain't been much good in the past. Don't know why it be much good in the future."

"Kate, I know things have happened to you, but I doubt those same things will happen with Urias. He seems to be a man of honor. Remember what I said to you about Mrs. Campbell and how he took care of her needs?"

Kate nodded.

"That same man is still in there. Whatever happened for him to lose Bullet has to be a deep wound. Those take time to heal."

"You're defending him?" Kate gasped.

"I suppose I am. I came to know Urias on the trail. He is not the same man we talked with last night or this morning. Whatever it is, we need to give him some time to work it all out."

"I know he's my kin, but I don't know him and I don't trust any man. I can't."

"Then let me do the trusting for the both of us. Things will work out." Prudence fired another prayer toward heaven. *Please, Lord, make everything work out. Don't let Kate suffer too much longer. She needs to know people care about her and love her. I know Urias does, even if he has a funny way of showing it to folks. I can't begin to understand why he wants me to be his bond servant, but if that is what I must do for Kate, then I'll do it.*

"You're praying, ain't ya?" Kate asked from behind her on the horse.

"Yes," Prudence admitted.

They continued on in silence, three people bound together by love and family, yet separated by the very same things. Prudence wanted to cry. Her heart ached. She didn't know what she'd done to bring about Urias's wrath or why he would hold her to her father's debts, but she'd done something to trigger his behavior. At least, it gave that appearance.

They traveled this way for days, barely talking one with the other. This time the journey was uneventful, unlike the last trip and the numerous events they'd endured while bringing the hogs down to the Cumberland Gap. When they arrived on the tenth day at Jamestown, Prudence couldn't believe her eyes. The house was large and well cared for. There was a smaller single-story house also set on the property, which she assumed was Urias's adoptive grandparents' home that he'd told her about building with his father.

"Urias," cried a small, black-haired boy, who ran out to greet them.

Urias caught the child in his arms and swung him up in the air. "Good to see you, Nash."

A small group of people gathered on the front porch.

Urias carried the youngster to the porch. "Mom, Dad, it's good to see you." Urias came up to the couple and gave them each a hug and a kiss.

Prudence looked over at Kate, who also appeared to feel out of place.

"You found her!" Mrs. MacKenneth stepped off the porch and went right over to Kate. "Welcome to our home, Katherine. We've been waiting and praying for you for a long time."

"Where's Bullet, Son?" Mr. MacKenneth asked.

Urias glanced over at Prudence, then back to his father. "It's a long story. I'll tell ya later."

"And who might you be?" Mrs. MacKenneth asked in a gentle voice.

Kate stood rigidly in place as their attention turned to Prudence.

"I'm—"

"She's my wife," Urias said, cutting her off. "In name only. It has to do with Bullet."

Mrs. MacKenneth paused for a moment, then opened her arms and embraced Prudence. "Welcome to the family."

Unable to respond, Prudence stood there just like Kate had done a few moments prior.

"Mom, the ladies would probably like to freshen up and get off their feet. They've been walking for miles. We pushed to get here before nightfall."

"Oh, certainly, do come in. Where are my manners?" Mrs. MacKenneth asked no one in particular.

Mac, as Urias had referred to him on more than one occasion, cleared his throat. "You ladies go freshen up a bit. Urias and I can take care of the horse and baggage."

Kate and Prudence glanced at each other, following Mrs. MacKenneth into the house. It was decorated with nice furnishings—nothing from a fancy cabinetmaker, but all looking extremely homey and functional.

"Come. Follow me. I'll set you up a warm pitcher of water to clean with and some fresh towels. Would you like to change your dresses as well?"

"Thank you. That would be wonderful, Mrs. MacKenneth." Prudence spoke up first.

"Please call me Pam. And my husband goes by Mac."

"Thank you. . .Pam. I can prepare the water," Kate offered.

"Nonsense. Tonight you're guests. Tomorrow you'll be family and given your own lot of chores to be done. Urias's room is at the top of the stairs, second door on the right. Make yourselves at home, and I'll bring up some warm water."

Prudence took the lead. Kate seemed too unsure of herself.

Prudence took Kate by the hand and led her up the stairs. "Come on. I can't wait to get this dress off."

Kate giggled.

They found the second room on the right and opened the door. Inside they found a room filled with books and hand drawings of horses. Prudence could smell Urias's compelling scent in the air. "This is his room," she blurted out.

"How do you know?"

Prudence pointed to a framed sketch on top of the dresser. "That's a picture of Bullet. Can't you tell?"

"If you say so. A horse is a horse, and they all look the same to me."

Pam came into the room carrying a pitcher of water and a kettle. "I brought up a second pitcher. I figured with two of you, you'll be needing more. I know when I come off the road, one pitcher is barely enough to hold me over before I can take a bath. I'll have Mac and Urias set up the tub for a hot bath tonight."

"I wouldn't want to impose." Prudence hoped Pam wouldn't take back her offer. A hot bath would be perfect.

"Nonsense. It's no trouble. Besides, Urias will need one as well. He'll get the tub after you two." Pam winked.

Kate giggled again.

Prudence smiled. Pam was everything Urias said she would be and more.

"Now, which one of you is going to tell me how it is that you married my son?"

fifteen

All right, Son, out with it. What happened?" Mac asked.

"It's a long story. Our mother sold Katherine as a bond servant. Her latest owner was Hiram Greene, Prudence's father. Hiram wanted me to pay her bond before he'd release Katherine. Prudence told me of a way to earn the money without having to come home and ask you for it. While she was explaining her idea to me in the barn, her father came out. He insisted that we marry after we were caught speaking to one another again later that night. He said I had dishonored his daughter."

Mac leaned back against the rail of the horse's pen. "And you agreed to this?"

"I was forced. He said he wouldn't sell Katherine's bond to me unless I married his daughter."

"You should have come home and talked with us. I would have paid Hiram Greene a visit."

Urias chuckled. His father was larger than life in most men's eyes. There was little doubt Mac would have put some fear into Hiram Greene.

"Prudence said we could get the marriage annulled since we haven't been as man and wife."

His father crossed his arms in front of his chest.

"So, you sold Bullet to pay for your sister's bond?"

"Not exactly. Prudence and I bought some hogs and ran them down to the Cumberland Gap. Oh, by the way, you should know that Mr. Campbell passed away. I helped Mrs. Campbell for a couple days, but her daughter came and fetched her by the time I returned from selling the hogs."

"I'm sorry to hear of Mrs. Campbell's loss, but you can tell me more on that matter, later. Tell me how it is that you had to sell Bullet."

Urias pulled in a deep breath and let it out slowly. "Hiram Greene has a gambling problem. While we were at Mrs. Campbell's farm, a rider came up and delivered a message to me from Mr. Greene saying I now owed him the price of a dowry for Prudence. Truthfully, the money I made from selling the hogs covered both Katherine's bond and Prudence's dowry, but when we arrived back at Hazel Green, we found Mr. and Mrs. Greene tied and bound to a chair and unconscious. Their servants were scattered throughout the house in the same state."

Mac combed his hands through his long hair.

"Mr. Greene confessed that he owed a man the money I was to pay him, plus a bit more for a gambling debt. Since I'm married to his daughter, even though in name only, I felt an obligation to pay the man's debt. When I got to the house of the person to whom Mr. Greene owed the debt, I discovered the debt was much higher and that he would not take a partial payment. He wanted it paid in full or not at all. We came to an understanding, and I gave him Bullet. Since the debt came from gambling on horse racing, I figured Bullet would be an acceptable bartering tool. He was."

"That was an honorable thing to do, Son. And a hard sacrifice. But what are you going to do about your wife?"

"I don't know. I don't want her to live in that house with Mr. Greene. They've not appreciated her. And to force their daughter to marry a stranger. . .well, it just seemed wrong to me. But I've done something foolish. At least, I hope it was foolish."

His father let out a half chuckle. "You mean more than what you've told me so far?"

"Guilty. I should have come home and sought your counsel, but Prudence's idea made so much sense. And I wanted to be a man and take care of my sister."

"I understand, Son. Go on. Tell me what else is wrong."

"After I came back from paying off Mr. Greene's debt, Prudence offered to get an annulment right away. I suspected, and still do, that she and her father conspired together. Was this their plan all along?"

Mac rubbed the back of his neck. "You know, Son, I couldn't say. I don't know these people. I'm afraid this is something you're going to have to come to terms with." He studied Urias a moment, then added, "There's more, isn't there?"

"Yes." Urias felt heat rush to his cheeks. "I told Prudence she was to be my bond servant to pay for her father's debt."

"You're going to have to work harder on tempering your impulsiveness, Son. I don't want you owning anyone, slave or bond servant. You can tell the woman she's not in debt to you and take it from there."

"Yes, sir. I've been trying to tell her for the past ten days on the trail home. But there's never been the right moment. We've talked little since we left Hazel Green. Even my own sister doesn't talk with me. Prudence says Katherine wasn't treated well by some of her previous bond owners."

Mac laid his hand upon Urias's shoulder. "I'm sorry, Son. I'll fill your mother in after we're down for the night. I expect she'll want to move Sarah into Molly's room tonight to make room for Katherine until you build your new home next spring."

"You can put Katherine and Prudence in my room. I'll bunk in the barn or on the sofa on really cold nights."

Mac gazed into Urias's eyes. "That will be fine. I'll want to hear more about this, but for now, what you've said is sufficient. We can chop down some trees for your house, and we'll spend more time on this matter, alone and away from everyone. I'm sure you have your reasons for suspecting Prudence, and you may be right. But if that were the case, why would she come here willingly?"

~

Prudence tried not to toss and turn too much in the bed. Everywhere she placed her head, she could smell Urias. She could see him in his artwork, in the items scattered throughout his room, and the books on the shelves. The titles alone were enough to tell about him.

The worst thing of all was that he had asked her to speak with him privately in the morning, to join him in the barn where he'd be milking the cows.

Pam had tried to break the tension in the air when Urias and Mac came in from the barn. It seemed hopeless. The children were the only cure. They talked and talked, asking question after question. Thankfully, they were mostly aimed at Urias.

There was little doubt in her mind that Urias had told Mac about the circumstances that led to her becoming Urias's wife. Prudence felt certain her version to Pam was far shorter than Urias's to his father. Neither parent seemed happy about her presence in the house, and Kate was no help. She was so afraid these people would treat her as a servant, she hardly said a word.

Urias answered all of his younger siblings' questions and even entertained them with a tale of swimming the hogs across the Cumberland River. Prudence could picture it clearly. She hadn't been with him at that point of the trip, but every time he mentioned it, she wished she had been. Staying with Mrs. Campbell had been a blessing, yet it had begun the separation between Urias and herself. Prior to that, they had begun to trust one another.

The memory of their kiss bored a hole in the pit of her stomach. The friendliness, or even a mild effort of being communicative, vanished after Urias sold Bullet. More than anything, Prudence wished she could have gone with Urias to meet with Sawyer Bishop. Had he taken advantage of Urias? Or was there more to her father's debt than a simple gambling wager? No one would leave people tied to chairs for a simple debt, would they? Wouldn't it be easier to have brought Father to court and sue him for the monies owed? Did money owed in a gambling debt constitute no debt at all in a court of law?

Prudence tossed again.

"Will you stay still!" Kate whispered.

"Sorry."

Prudence shared the bed with Kate. There was ample room for the two of them, and even if she could sleep, she'd still be bothered by Kate's tossing and turning.

"I be up all night with this here strange bed. I ain't never slept on anything like it before," Kate whispered.

Prudence hadn't thought about the bed, its size, or the firmness of the mattress. It was firmer than most she'd slept on before, but if Urias could sleep on the ground with no worries, perhaps a firm mattress was more to his liking. Personally, she enjoyed a medium state of firmness. Not too soft and not too hard. "It's better than the ground."

"Aye, that it is." There was a moment of silence, then Kate started chatting on about the house and the strangers in it. "And Urias is so at home with these people."

"Yes, he seems quite content. Those children really love him."

"Aye. Babes they are. Every one of them. But they love Urias and treat him like a big brother."

"Yes." Prudence had often wondered what it would be like

to have an older brother. "Kate, did you like having an older brother?"

"Ain't never thought about it. I suppose it be so. Urias was always there, looking out for me." Kate rolled on her side and faced Prudence. "Pru, how long do you think you'll be Urias's bond servant? Can a man do that to his legal wife?"

❧

Urias spent most of the evening making the loft habitable, eventually building a bed out of fresh hay and covering it with some canvas, then a sheet. Perhaps he should ask his grandparents if he could sleep on their sofa by the woodstove. Winter hadn't settled in yet, and already the wind howled through the barn.

Who was he kidding? It wasn't his bed or the place he was sleeping that kept him awake, but rather the possible scenarios of how to deal with Prudence. Should he take her to Creelsboro, where she could find a job and they could find an attorney to annul their marriage? Or should he have her work off some of her father's debt? Not as a servant but. . .but what? Urias couldn't afford to pay her and have a portion of her salary go toward the debt—which, his conscience reminded him, he'd told Hiram Greene was a gift. *That was before I knew what it would cost me.* He didn't have an income of his own, and without Bullet, it would be awhile longer before he could begin breeding horses as a profitable business.

Urias glanced down at the pair of horses he had bred, of which Bullet was the product. They were a fine pair. The wild stallion didn't care to be penned in. He seldom stayed still in the stall. Most of the time, Urias kept him out in the corral, but he wanted the stallion to get used to being in the barn before winter. The mare was expecting once again, but it would be a couple years before he could ride that horse. He glanced to the right, where a yearling stood. Its lines were similar to Bullet's but not quite as powerful. She would be a good breeder like her mother.

Closing his eyes, he tried to go to sleep. He continued to ignore the nagging feeling that wanted to bring up the anger he felt toward Hiram Greene and Prudence and how they'd tricked him into paying their debts. He knew it was wrong to be angry, that he needed to forgive, but neither had asked for forgiveness.

Prudence apologized for her father, he mused, then shook off the memory. He would not be fooled by the beauty of Prudence Greene, by the gentle way she spoke, or her so-called love for his sister. She was like her father, he reminded himself over and over again.

ᴥ

Morning came early, along with the body aches from lack of sleep. Urias stretched and milked the cow.

"Morning, Son." His father walked in. "Good to have your helping hands around here. Now, tell me about these hogs."

Urias went into a detailed description of his and Prudence's trip with the hogs and about their stay with Mrs. Campbell.

"You've had quite the adventure. Did you really need to swim the hogs across the river?"

"Only to save money. By that point Mr. Greene had passed along his demand for a dowry payment."

His father leaned against the stall's planks. "Seems to me if Prudence was aware of her father's debt, she wouldn't have put herself out and traveled with you."

"That's what doesn't make sense. I've asked her to come speak with me this morning. I have a mind to absolve her from the debt, but the matter of our marriage is still an issue."

"Son, I'm not going to presume to know what the answer is on this one. Seems to me a man really is married if he marries a woman, even if he marries her in name only. It also seems to me that the good Lord doesn't take to marriage as being a conveyance. If you vowed to God to marry this woman, you are married."

"It wasn't a real wedding—just some rushed together service in her father's office."

"I see. And doesn't the Bible speak about obeying the laws of the land?"

"But. . ." Urias's shoulders slumped under the pressure.

His father came up beside him and laid a hand on his shoulder. "I understand your not wanting to take her as your wife. But if you gave your word, you might just have to live with it."

Urias swallowed hard. He had fully intended to make Prudence his wife when he said his vows. He didn't even think or know about an annulment until Prudence mentioned it. He'd given his word. Like it or not, Prudence was his wife.

"Pray on the matter, Son. This afternoon, let's go fell some trees for your house."

If he worked quickly, Urias knew he could get the foundation done before the frost set in for the winter. "Yes, I imagine we won't be able to build until spring."

"Depends on the winter. But we'll do what we can before the weather turns bitter."

He finished milking the cow and handed the bucket to his father. "I'm going to spend some time with the Lord before I speak with Prudence."

Mac squeezed his shoulder. "I know you'll do the right thing."

But do I want to do the right thing? Urias wondered. *Is it right for a man to be bound to another person who doesn't really love you? Who used you?*

Falling on his knees, he pleaded with the Lord for some understanding of what to do. After an hour, he heard Prudence call, "Urias? Where are you?"

He got up and went to the edge of the loft. "Up here."

"Should I come up?" she asked.

He glanced back at his hay bed. Apart from that, there was nothing to sit down on. "I'll be right down."

He climbed down and prayed once again. As he walked toward her, he could see her fear. "I want to apologize for insisting that you become my bond servant. I was angry, and I took it out on you."

Prudence nibbled her lower lip and looked down at her feet, giving a slight nod.

"I am not going to require you to pay back your father's debt."

She looked up at him with her big brown eyes. Urias swallowed. "I've decided to honor our marriage and keep you as my wife."

Her eyes widened. "All right," she stammered.

sixteen

Prudence didn't know what to say to Urias when he said he intended to honor their marriage. Now, three months later, she still didn't understand what that meant. She worked night and day helping out with the children, the house, and even working with Urias on his new house. The exterior walls were up, but they hadn't been able to do any work on it for the past six weeks. The winter winds made it too cold.

But what did it mean to be husband and wife when you were nothing more than strangers? They still hadn't spent any time alone with one another, and she still stayed with Kate. Kate, on the other hand, was no longer afraid. She felt comfortable with the MacKenneths. It was a blessing to see her free. But Kate's freedom only magnified Prudence's entrapment. The marriage had been to help Kate, but still they had no real life together. She loved Urias and how he treated others, but he constantly avoided her.

Today things would be different. Today she would confront him and suggest they annul the marriage. She couldn't live like this. Even life in her parents' home was not like the loneliness she felt living in Urias's home.

Prudence marched up to Urias's house. She had seen him leave to take advantage of the break in the weather. "Urias?" she called.

"In the back room," he answered.

It wasn't that he was unfriendly, but they never had time alone. They did not behave as married people. "Urias, there's something we should talk about."

"Sure." He brushed the sawdust off his handmade leather pants.

Her stomach flipped at the sight of him.

"What would you like to talk about?"

"Us."

His face reddened. "What about us?"

"Urias, I can't go on like this. I feel I don't belong here. I feel I don't belong anywhere."

"I see."

"No, I don't believe you do."

Urias looked down at what he'd been working on. Prudence followed his line of vision. *A bed.*

"Prudence, I know I'm not much of a husband, but I can't escape how we got married. I was forced to marry you."

"I'm fully aware."

He closed the distance between them. "No, you don't understand. I promised I'd take care of you, but I can't get past the manipulation. Did you or did you not work with your father to have me pay off his debts?"

"What?" She stepped back from him. "Is that what this has been all about? You think I knew of my father's gambling debts? You think I set you up to pay him off? Are you forgetting something?"

"Your helping me with the hogs. I know," he finished her thoughts.

"Exactly. Why would I do that if I were working with my father?"

"For the dowry," he said in blunt response.

Dowry. She'd forgotten her father's additional request. "I see. Well, in that case, I wish for you to make me your bond servant again so I can pay off my father's debt, and once that's paid off, I'll be free to leave."

"Is that what you want?"

No, she wanted to scream. She wanted her husband, a real marriage. She wanted to be able to love Urias and feel the comfort of his embrace once again.

"Prudence, I don't want you to owe me anything." He looked back at the bed frame he was working on. "You're free to leave. I will not hold you here."

"What about our marriage?" she asked.

"Do what you would like on the matter. I'll sign any papers you would have me sign." He brushed past her. "Excuse me." He left her standing there alone in the room. On the floor was the headboard for a bed. A bed for two.

જ

Prudence's words still burned in his ears. He went out to the back woods. There was nothing like chopping down a tree to work off your anger. He'd been making their bed. How could he have been so foolish? Of course, she didn't want to be married to him—not for real.

With each passing day, he'd watched her. He'd watched the way she played with the children and helped around the house. He had to admit he'd been keeping her at a distance, unsure of what to do and how to go about it. He thought if he put together their bedroom, he'd have an opportunity to explain that he really did want to make this a real marriage, not in name only, as it had been for the past four months.

Now she was going. She didn't really care for him, did she?

For the past month, his father and mother had been giving him lectures on how he treated Prudence unfairly. They were right. He'd been treating her more like a visitor to his home— a temporary visitor who had overstayed her welcome. But Prudence hadn't overstayed, had she? He'd told her what to do and when to do it since they'd first met.

Life had been different on the trail, where they talked as equals, working together to bring the hogs to the Cumberland

Gap. When it had been just the two of them. If they had stayed on the trail for a day or two longer, he would have made her his wife in all the ways that a husband and wife become one. But that hadn't happened. Instead, they came upon her parents, tied and gagged. He'd met with Sawyer Bishop and paid off Hiram Greene's debt. He thought back on the conversation with Bishop that caused Urias to start wondering about Prudence's true intentions. Had he misjudged her?

Urias planted the ax in the tree and walked back to the cabin. "Prudence?" he called out.

He ran into the house, but she was gone.

He ran to the large farmhouse. "Mom, have you seen Prudence?"

"No. She left awhile ago, looking for you."

"She found me. If you see her again, would you tell her that I'm looking for her?"

"Yes. Is everything all right?"

"No, but it will be."

Urias ran out to the barn. His mare was missing. "Where did she go?" He mounted the stallion and tracked her heading to Creelsboro. Before long, he caught up to her, riding the mare without a thought in the world.

"Prudence," he called.

She turned around. "Urias?"

"Stop," he ordered. "Please." He softened his tone.

She halted the horse.

"Prudence, I don't want you to leave."

"Why?" Tears began to fall from her already red and swollen eyes.

Urias's gut tightened. "Because I want our marriage to work."

"Why?"

Urias closed his eyes. Why did he want their marriage to

work? "Because I want us to get back to the trail. I want us to try to be the people we were on the trail."

"I haven't changed."

Urias looked down at the reins in his hands, then looked up at her. "Prudence, Sawyer Bishop told me that your father had tried to pay him off once before."

"Oh?"

"He said your father offered to give you to Sawyer as his mistress to pay off the debt."

"He did *what?*" Prudence's face reddened with anger. "So this is why you believed I was in on some scheme with my father?"

"Yes, I'm ashamed to say. Can you forgive me?"

"Forgive you? I want to—"

"I'm sorry, Prudence."

"The more I learn of his business dealings, the more ashamed I am of my father. He tried to sell me?"

"That's what Sawyer said, although I don't know that his word is any more trustworthy than your father's." Urias dismounted and reached up to Prudence, encouraging her to come down from the saddle. "Let's sit down over here." He pointed to a browned grassy hill.

Prudence started to cry all over again. He held her in his arms, taking in the sweet fragrance that was her unique scent. He'd missed that. After a few moments, he lifted her face and pushed back a few strands of hair. "Can we start over?"

"Why would you want to?" she sniffled.

Urias smiled. There was hope. "Because I'd like to get to know my wife, the real woman, not the image I've concocted in my mind based on what others have said and done."

A slight smile edged up the corners of her mouth. "I'd like that."

Unable to let the moment slip through his hands, he pulled

her close and kissed her. As with their first kiss, their passions ignited. Urias pulled back first. "Honey, I. . .I mean, we can't."

She knitted her eyebrows, and a delicate wrinkle formed in the center of her forehead.

"What I'm trying to say—and doing a miserable job of it—is that if we are to be man and wife, I don't want it to be because of our marriage at your parents' house. I want us to be married in my church, with God's blessing."

A smile lit up her face. "I'd like that, too."

"So would I. But first, let's wait a bit and make certain this is what we both want."

"Urias? Can I be perfectly honest with you?"

His heart thundered in his chest. "Yes."

"I've been in love with you since we were on the trail."

"Really?" Urias beamed.

"Yes. It must be those green eyes."

Urias wiggled his eyebrows. "Mom always said my wife would fall in love with them. When you're a teen with my coloring, you're made fun of—a lot."

"I think you're rather handsome." Prudence blushed.

Urias leaned forward. Prudence blocked his lips with her fingers. Why she was stopping the kiss made no real sense, even to her, except that they both had said they wanted to wait and have a real wedding.

Urias leaned back. "You're right. We'll need to take this slowly."

"Urias, if we're to be husband and wife, am I to strictly follow your orders, or do I have a say in matters?"

Urias chuckled, then picked up a small twig. "I want to hear your opinions. I valued your advice and insight on the trail. I just couldn't get past my anger."

"You had a right to be angry. But wouldn't it have been wiser to speak with me about it?"

"Perhaps. But under the circumstances, I doubt I would have trusted your word any more than that of any other stranger," he said.

"Ouch."

"I'm sorry, but we need to be honest. I don't want there to be any further secrets between us."

"Agreed." Prudence sat back, balancing herself on her elbows. She looked up at the sky. "Do you think winter will end soon?"

"I hope so. I want to get our house done."

"Will Kate be moving in with us?" Prudence could feel the heat rise on her cheeks.

"I'll have to speak with my parents. If they're agreeable to let her keep my old room, then I don't see why she would need to stay with us. At least not at first. I'm torn, Prudence. I want Katherine to feel like the place is hers but. . ."

"Will she ever feel that way about any place?"

"Exactly. She and I have talked some. She's still pretty angry with God, but she's coming around. I can't say that I blame her for feeling bitter, considering some of the things she's gone through."

"I know. She said that it's hard to believe in a loving and compassionate God when she's seen so little evidence in her own life. Part of what attracted me to you in the beginning, Urias, was watching you live out your faith. However, I was beginning to question your faith in the past couple of months."

"Ouch." Urias chuckled.

"You said, be honest."

"That I did. And I can't say I blame you for wondering. It bothered me to sell Bullet, but that was minor compared to what I thought you had been a part of."

"Do you really think my father would have sold me?"

"I honestly don't know. He certainly was a desperate man."

"He was getting more and more upset with my not producing a suitor, and all the men I discussed finances with seemed to think I had two heads. But you never did. That's another thing that attracted me to you, I might add."

"I love how you sacrificed yourself for a friend. When I saw your feet all marred up on the trail and your not complaining about it, I thought to myself, 'she's an amazing woman.'"

Prudence smiled. "Where do we go from here?"

seventeen

Shaking off the dust and pieces of dried grass was easy compared to the shakes in his legs. He'd just committed to Prudence, even asking her to remarry him. If only he could get his stomach to relax. He opened his hand and offered it to Prudence. She slipped her delicate fingers into his rough, open palm. Again he fought down a surge of trembling born of emotions that threatened to overwhelm him whenever they were close. She loved him. She'd loved him for a while, and he'd never known it.

He scrutinized the fine lines of her face. Was she shaky as well? "Nervous?"

"Terrified. Are you sure?"

He nodded, not trusting himself to speak.

"That sure, huh?"

He swallowed the lump in his throat and spoke. "Honey, I'm unsure what to say, how to act around you."

"Be yourself, Urias. That's the man I fell in love with."

"I can do that." But could he tell her that he loved her? Did he love her? Or was there a part of him just trying to make do with a situation that he'd gotten himself into without thinking, just reacting?

He helped her up to her horse. She felt wonderful in his hands. There was a connection between them, but would it last?

"I think you're right about waiting awhile, Urias. Let's make sure we're doing the right thing this time."

"Yes. How long do you want to wait?" he asked and mounted his horse.

146

"For spring? Summer?" she suggested.

"I should have most of the house ready by spring. We can aim for that."

"What about your parents? What will they think about all this?"

That I should have done this a long time ago. "They like you, Prudence. They'll be fine with our choice. It's a sensible one, don't you think?"

"Yes, but. . ."

He lifted his reins and waited for her to continue. She went no further. Should he pry? There was the matter of not keeping secrets one from the other, but did that include all of your innermost thoughts? "But?"

"Nothing, really."

"Do you have doubts about our getting married—I mean a real marriage?"

She looked away from him and up the hill at an outcropping of granite protruding at an odd angle from the steep slope. He'd never noticed that before.

"Yes, there's a part of me that would like to be married. Then there's a part of me that has wrestled with our marriage having been the most regrettable decision I've ever made."

Ouch. She's really being honest. "I've wrestled with the same, but, given the same circumstances, I'm not sure I would have done it differently."

"Kate needed our help."

"Agreed. But our marriage, if there is to be a real marriage, can't be based on what anyone else needs or wants."

"That's my point. If we are to truly have a real marriage, we ought to at least start by courting. I mean. . .I realize we've been living in the same house and have spent numerous days on the trail together but. . ."

Urias hadn't thought about courting. They were married already. The church wedding wasn't even required, legally, although he felt in his heart it was necessary. But courting—does a man really have to go through all those fancy steps? *She's already said she loves me,* he argued with himself.

"If you're thinkin' what I think you're thinkin', that's exactly why we need to court."

"Huh?" Urias scratched the back of his neck. "I don't get it. We're already married. Why would I need to. . ." He caught himself before he set a waterfall in motion. He was missing something here, he knew. She knew it, too, and it wasn't likely she'd tell him. He'd have to figure this out on his own somehow.

"I don't think we should make any marriage plans."

Urias shook his head, blinked, and kept himself from sticking his finger in his ear to see if he truly had heard what he thought he heard. "But I thought we just settled that we'd aim to get married in the spring."

She wasn't going to give him a hint of what was on her mind, he realized, and at the moment, he wanted to be upset with her for not telling him. Instead, he found himself wondering what he didn't understand and why it was so important to her to be courted.

"Urias." She reached over and placed her hand upon his. "I'll go back to the house with you, where we can think about this for a few days. Is that fair?"

He nodded, not sure what he had done to cause this change in plans. Hadn't she just confessed her love for him? Didn't they just share a tender and passionate kiss? What more is there? *I even told her I wanted to get the marriage right and marry in front of You, Lord. Please help me out here.*

The world was silent. A cardinal—male, judging by its brightly colored feathers—perched on a tree and sang out loud and shrill. Was he laughing at Urias not understanding or simply trying to tell what the answer was? In either case, Urias didn't know, so he waited for Prudence to turn her horse around before he turned his. They headed back to the farm together, but even more distant than they had been for the past three months.

What have I done now?

a.

Prudence fought down her anger. She wouldn't tell Urias what she longed to hear him say. She wanted him to treat her as if she had worth to him. She wanted to be cherished, at least just a little bit. She knew it would take years before Urias would ever confess his love for her, but he could show some respect. *I guess that's why I want him to court me, Lord. Am I wrong? Am I expecting too much from a man, from Urias? Shouldn't a wife be treasured? At least in a little way?* she prayed.

"Prudence," Urias called out as his horse trotted up to her. "What's wrong? Forgive me for being ignorant, but I honestly don't know what I've done this time."

Prudence gently pulled back on the reins. She scanned his wonderful green eyes, pleading for her understanding. "A woman," she stammered, looking for the right words. "Me—I really don't want a marriage just for the sake of a marriage. I want to know that my husband cares for me."

"I care," he defended.

"Urias, look at your parents. They love one another. They show it in the little things they say and do for one another. I'm not saying I'm expecting you to love me like that. I know that our marriage will always have the blackened past of how we began as husband and wife. But. . ."

Urias climbed down off his horse and came up beside her, reaching up for her. "Come on." He held up his arms. "We have more to talk about."

She wanted to fall into his embrace but stayed firmly planted in her saddle. "Wouldn't it be best to give us a couple days to think about this?"

"No, I think we need to talk more. I've upset you. I've

apparently said some things wrong. We need to clarify everything in order to be able to think for a while. If'n you need some time to think after we have a clear understanding of our future, that would be fine."

Prudence released the reins and slid into his proffered embrace.

"That's better. Now, the Good Book says we ought not to let the sun go down on our anger."

"The Good Book also says husbands are to love their wives. Should we be married if you don't?"

"I do love you. I mean," he stammered, "I think this love can grow, but it'll need time."

He loves me. Prudence held back a smile. "What kind of love do you have for me?"

He sat on the ground and waited for her to join him. "Most of the time, it's love one shows another person. I don't want to see anything bad happen to you. I feel a sense of duty to protect you. Not really duty—I don't know if I can explain it. It's kinda like my father's protective love for his family, but I know it isn't as strong as that. However, if anyone tried to hurt you, I would fight for you. I will protect you."

Prudence took in a deep breath. *It's a start.*

"You say you love me, Prudence, but how do you know it's the love a wife should have for a husband? How do you know it isn't just physical attraction? We both have to admit, there is a powerful attraction between us."

The heat of a deep blush spread across her cheeks and down her neck. "I don't know why or how I love you. I know it doesn't make much sense. It's little things, really. . . . How you care for Kate. . . How you sacrificed for her. How you treated Mrs. Campbell and others on the trail. There's a million little things you've done that make me think I love you. I guess that's why it's so hard to stay living here, knowing you don't care for me in the same way."

Urias chuckled. "There's a ton of little things that I love and admire about you, too. It's the way you are with the children, the way you sacrificed for Katherine, and the way you help others and give of yourself. Even the way your mind works with numbers—to name a few."

She held back the tears.

Urias leaned over and faced her, their noses less than an inch apart. "You need to hear these things, don't you?"

She nodded.

"You're a beautiful woman, Prudence, inside and out. I'll admit I don't know if the passion I feel is the basis for the deep love a man and wife should share, but I believe God will honor us if we honor Him. I'm willing to work on being a good husband if you're willing to work on being a good wife."

"What do you want in a wife?" she asked, silently praying it was more than her father wanted from his wife yet less than some of the things he'd grown to expect from her mother over the years.

"That's a hard one. I want your help in financial matters, and I think together we can build a good farm for breeding horses. But I want you to be willing to make me talk when I want to be alone. Sometimes I'll need to be alone, but somehow I need my wife to be able to figure out when those times are. I'm like my dad in that respect. I can spend weeks at a time away from anyone and be very happy. Mom will be able to help you understand how to keep me from my shell of solitude. Oh, and my wife needs to cook." He wiggled his eyebrows.

"I think I can do that."

"I know you can." Urias reached over and traced his thumb across her jawline. "Daily kisses from my wife would be another good thing."

She swatted his hand. "You've had your daily limit."

Urias let out a guttural laugh. "I didn't say a single kiss, my dear. I said kisses."

Urias planed down the rough wood to put the finishing touches on his and Prudence's bed. It would be his wedding present to her. Unfortunately, she'd seen it the day he proposed to her. Courting Prudence turned out to be a good thing, he decided. They were learning more and more about one another, and the desire to be married to Prudence grew steadily each day. The wedding had been planned for one month from now, and he had precious little time to finish the house. Katherine had decided to stay in the big farmhouse and help Pam with the children. Mom was expecting another child and was having a difficult time getting around. Katherine saw she was truly needed and appreciated being asked to help out.

If the Lord blesses, Urias pondered, *hopefully Katherine will someday help Prudence in the same situation.*

"Urias," Prudence called out.

"Stay put," he ordered and covered the bed frame with a piece of canvas. He went out and found her in the newly finished kitchen.

"Hi." She looked down at her feet. A sure sign he was in for a special treat.

"Hi." He closed the gap between them. "Did I tell you how beautiful you look this morning?"

Prudence blushed.

An ever-deepening sense of love, honor, and how unique Prudence Greene O'Leary truly was swept over him anew. Daily he was learning to appreciate her sacrificial love, no longer just for Katherine, but for himself and others, as well. She was a gift from the Lord. Colossians 3:19, a verse his father challenged him on—"Husbands, love your wives, and be not bitter against them"—rang through his mind one more time. Was there any bitterness left in him regarding Prudence and her father's deception? He'd long ago realized

Prudence had no part in the deceptions of her father. And he even had some grace to extend to Hiram Greene, knowing how hard it would be to admit to his wife and family that he'd made a terrible mistake.

"What's the matter?" she asked.

"Nothing."

She placed her hands on her hips. "You're not being honest with me. I thought we agreed no more secrets," she challenged.

"I'm sorry. But must a man tell his wife everything he is thinking?"

"Perhaps not everything. The reason I came over was to try to persuade you to join me in a picnic."

"Picnic?" Urias looked for a basket of food. Prudence's cooking continued to whet his appetite. She'd been taking lessons from his mother and grandmother, as well as Kate. "It's not that warm out—unless you were thinking of eating in here."

"No, I had another place in mind."

"Oh?" Clearly, she'd been planning something special. Desire wanted him to say yes. Reality won the day. "I do have a lot of work to do." He paused, then added, "If I'm to have this house done by the time we're married."

Her shoulders slumped. She put on a fake smile. "I understand. What can I do to help?" She scanned the kitchen. The cabinets were done. The counter and wood sink were in place.

Urias had ordered a couple cast-iron stoves, which were expected to be in later this week. The stone floor was a safety feature he'd learned about from his father that would limit household fires from indoor cooking. The empty space where the stove belonged was a reminder of work still not done.

"Honey, I'd really like to take off the afternoon and spend it with you, but we have to keep our focus if this place is to be ready by the time we're to be married."

"I know you're right. It's just that. . ." She let her words trail off as she glanced into the main living room of the house. Her posture changed, and she locked her gaze on his. "I've been thinking about the horse breeding and wanted to discuss it with you."

Since their hog expedition, there hadn't been much in the discussion of finances. In part, Urias felt it was due to the business with her father's debt. "What do you have on your mind?"

"I was trying to calculate how much hay one needs to store up for the winter in order to feed a horse. Which got me to thinking about how much space we'd need in a barn, especially once you have several expecting mares. How much land will we need for this grain? And is the land you've been given large enough for the plans you have?"

Urias rolled back on his heels. "You've been thinkin', all right. First, we don't have enough land to feed a lot of horses, yet. I've set my sights on a spread a few hours from here. I won't have the funds for an additional year with the loss of Bullet. I don't know if the land will still be available by then. If not, we can't go that large scale that quickly. We'll have to start off slow, build up some revenue, then make some purchase arrangements with various area farmers."

"What about the barn?"

"In my mind, I have a plan to build a series of stalls, making it a long, narrow barn with storage room in the loft."

"Where are you planning on building the barn, and when?"

Urias chuckled. "Next year. But it will be built in sections. It will grow as our needs grow."

She smiled.

I must have said something right, he reflected as he suppressed a grin.

eighteen

Urias sat with a sheet of paper, laying out all that he and Prudence had discussed earlier in the day, on his lap. The house was quiet. He turned up the wick of the kerosene lamp for a better view. He held up the paper. "This is amazing, Prudence. You've put everything down in writing."

It had taken courage to make such a bold overture in their relationship, but after their many discussions, she felt it was time to brave it and see if her husband would truly want her opinion about business matters.

"What's this here?" He pointed to an income column.

"Those are stud fees. I thought we might be able to make use of Bullet's father's service for others looking for a horse with good lines. He's a bit wild, but I think that fire will be helpful in pitching his worth."

"Hard to say. Some folks worry about their mares being beaten up by a wild male."

She nodded. She didn't know that could be a problem but instantly saw the point Urias was making.

"But it's a good idea for raising more capital." He scrutinized the paper a bit more. "What's this?"

Prudence giggled. "That's an idea for after the harvest. I was thinking. . ." How could she put this? "I was thinking, since the foal isn't due for some time, perhaps we could take another trip through the Cumberland Gap."

"Another trip?"

"Yes. I was thinking we did so well with the price of the hogs last time that it might be. . ."

Urias laughed out loud, then caught himself. "Honey, I

have no interest in hauling hogs over the trail ever again. If I have to, I will but. . ."

She'd had doubts about putting that suggestion down on paper, but the thousand dollars they earned the last time seemed like good pay for a couple weeks' work.

"Honey, I want to raise horses, not hogs," Urias finished.

"I suppose it wasn't that great of a suggestion."

"No, I'm not saying that." He reached out his hand and lifted her chin with his first finger.

"If we left from here, we could take a wagon," she pressed. It wasn't that she really wanted to be on the trail with the hogs again.

"This isn't about the pigs or making money, is it?" he asked.

"No," she confessed.

"Time alone?" he asked.

She nodded.

He put the paperwork aside. "Pru, I had in mind to take you away for a couple weeks after we got married. Just you and me. The problem is, it'll be the height of spring planting, and I'm needed here."

"I know. I understand."

He reached out to her. She kept her eyes fixed on his and took the final step that separated them. "What if we ran off to the minister now?" she whispered in his ear.

"What about the house?" He wrapped his arms around her.

She leaned in and placed her arms on his shoulders. She didn't care about the house, a fancy bed, or anything. She only wanted to be with Urias. They'd been husband and wife for five months, and she didn't want to wait any longer to be his wife in every way. "I love you, Urias. I—"

He placed his warm fingertip to her lips. "What about the plans everyone has made on our behalf? Hasn't Mom been working on a gown with you?"

She pushed back from his arms and nodded. "You're right," she admitted.

He pulled her back and held her tightly. His warm breath tickled her ear. "I love you, too, and I'd like nothing more than to be married tonight. But one of the things the Lord's been showing me is we're both impulsive by nature. We both jump, then look where we've fallen. As much as I hate to admit it, I think we were right in setting the wedding date for when we did."

She wanted to kiss him. She was afraid to kiss him. They were married, but they both agreed they wanted a marriage where God was placed at the center, not themselves. She laid her head on his shoulder. "I think the Lord's been telling me the same thing during my quiet time," she admitted.

"Tell you what we can do." He paused. "We can do our devotionals together. Perhaps not in the morning." He chuckled. She still struggled getting up as early as the rest of the household did. "But in the evening after dinner, we could spend some time in the Bible and prayer. What do you think?"

"I'd like that." Although if she was being perfectly honest, it wasn't what she had in mind for being alone with Urias.

"I think it will be a grand adventure. In some ways, we look at various issues in very different ways, but ultimately we still come to the same conclusions. We could have very spirited discussions from time to time, I would think." He winked.

"More than likely," she agreed. "Should we go over those figures some more?"

&

"Urias," Katherine called as the kitchen door slammed shut behind her.

"Katherine? What's the matter?"

"Nothing. Pam told Prudence you didn't want her to come to the house, so she sent me."

"How is she?"

"She's fine. If you call nervous fine. How are you?"

"Good."

"You've been working night and day." Katherine scanned the bedroom. "This is beautiful. She'll love it."

A smile rose on his face. He hoped Prudence would like it. If anyone would know her tastes, it would be Katherine. "I'm glad. I wanted to make the room special for her."

"You really like her, don't you?"

"She's a remarkable woman."

Katherine nodded, then sat down on the bed. "Pru asked me to check on you and to make sure you weren't too tired. She's worried about you."

"I'm fine. Tell her I'm anxiously awaiting the two more days."

Katherine smiled, then looked down at her lap. She laced her fingers together and released them a couple of times. Urias had learned long ago not to push Katherine—to let her have the time needed to collect her thoughts. He placed a loving hand on her shoulder. She didn't flinch. He silently praised the Lord.

She glanced up at him, her green eyes pooled with fresh tears. "I'm happy for Prudence. I'm glad you two are going to make a real marriage out of this horrible mess."

Urias sat down beside his sister. "Katherine, I love Prudence, and I want to be the best possible husband to her. I'm also here for you. I'll do anything I can to help you. Prudence and I both will."

"Do you really think God cares for me?"

"Yes. I know you've been through a horrible ordeal. I can only imagine what you went through. But God does love you, and He was always there. I know it doesn't make sense sometimes. We feel so lost and alone, like God has deserted us. And I can't begin to explain why God lets bad things happen to people. I remember from the Bible about Job and all he went through. I sometimes think about my situations and how horrific they seem at the time. Then I compare it with Job and what he went through and realize I haven't got it so bad."

"How could Mother sell me like that?"

"I don't know. She wasn't a well woman. We both know the drinking caused her to change. She must have been desperate for money and driven by the need for alcohol. That doesn't excuse her actions, just explains them. At least that's how I've come to look at it. I was mighty angry at Mother for what she did to you."

"You were?"

"Yup. I think I took it out on Prudence, which she didn't deserve."

"I don't recall you ever being real angry. I mean, I saw you upset, but you weren't punching or hitting anything. You never yelled."

"Katherine, I've learned to control my anger. I saw what it did with Mother. And I've seen what Mom and Dad have worked through when they are angry. The Bible says 'be ye angry, but sin not.' It took awhile, and I'm still working on it, but we can get angry and not sin."

"I want to believe like you, Prudence, and the MacKenneths, but I can't forgive God for letting it happen to me."

Urias's stomach tightened. He knew Katherine still didn't recognize that she had her own sins to seek God's forgiveness for—that it wasn't God who needed to be forgiven. This was not the time or place to press the point. "I understand. You were a child, an innocent child. Bad things should not happen to innocent children. But you weren't killed. There are many worse things that could have happened to you that didn't."

"I feel so dirty—so worthless," she confessed.

Urias took in a deep breath. "You were sinned against. God loves you, and He wants you to be free from the bondage of those who sinned against you."

"I want to be free, Urias. I truly do, but the memories come back to haunt me night after night."

He gently explained how to ask the Lord into her heart and how to rebuke evil thoughts when they came in. But he saw she wasn't ready to take that final step. He would continue to pray for Katherine's freedom from the past, as he knew he'd have to pray to be rid of the renewed anger within himself for the men who had abused his sister—as well as their mother for selling her into bondage.

"I love you, Katherine. I'm sorry those things happened to you."

"It's not your fault. I used to think it was. If you'd never left, nothing would have happened to me. But I don't know. She could have sold both of us, couldn't she?"

"I never thought about it, but you're right, she could have." Urias silently thanked the Lord for his salvation and for His grace in allowing him to run into the MacKenneths on the trail.

"I'll think about what you said. Maybe someday I'll be able to forgive God and accept His grace."

"I'm always here for you," he offered. "And so is He."

She gave a slight nod and left him sitting in the bedroom. Taking a moment to pray, he handed over his renewed anger and his sister, Katherine, to the Lord. Urias didn't have the answers for her. He couldn't explain why such awful things had happened to her. He knew precious little of what exactly transpired, but her demeanor and the few comments she'd let slip were enough to know that someone, at least one of the men who had owned her bond, had taken advantage of her. He was ever so grateful that Hiram Greene had purchased her. Urias caught himself at that thought. Yes, he was grateful to Hiram Greene. "Lord, You're amazing." Urias jumped to his feet and headed to his parents' house.

❧

Two more days, Prudence reminded herself. She and Urias

would be married, with God's blessing, in two more days. She couldn't wait. His news about being thankful for her father struck a chord. She hadn't forgiven him for how he'd handled Kate's bondage. Business or not, it wasn't right. Urias was right. Her father needed to be forgiven. *But how do I forgive my own father, who was willing to use his own flesh and blood for his own personal gain?*

She walked behind the house and up the small hill. She'd found the secluded place quite by accident one day and ever since had used it as a place to pray and gather her thoughts. The MacKenneth home was a large farmhouse, but with so many people, a place for solitude seemed very needed.

She sat down on a log that provided a perfect place for a moment's rest, closed her eyes, and began to pray. She never heard the approaching footsteps.

"Hello." Grandma MacKenneth smiled as she took her seat on the log beside Prudence. "Forgive me for intruding."

"It's all right," Prudence politely answered.

"I've seen you come a time or two and thought you might like a listening ear. If not, I'll be on my way once I catch my breath. How do you like this little spot?"

"It's wonderful." She realized she mustn't have been the only person who thought it was the ideal place for solitude.

"I've tried to keep it as natural as possible, but every now and again I'd have Timmon come up and pull some small bushes or trees that insisted on growing in the circle. That was before his accident, of course."

"Do you come up here often?"

"No, not too much anymore. Caring for Timmon requires a lot of my time."

"I understand."

"I'm getting on in years, so I'll just be frank. Do you love Urias?"

"Yes. But he isn't the reason I came up here."

"What seems to be troubling you?"

"My father. I'm sure you've heard."

She placed her hand lovingly on Prudence's knee. "A little. But why don't you tell me."

"You know the circumstances of how Urias and I were forced to marry and about Urias paying off my father's gambling debt."

"Yes. Go on."

"Well, the man he paid told Urias that my father had once offered me in exchange for his gambling losses. Had he accepted my father's offer, I would have become his mistress."

Prudence saw the compassion in the woman's eyes.

"I'm sorry. One doesn't like to learn that a parent or parents didn't cherish them. I may be wrong, but I think your father is sin sick. He's lost in the sin of his gambling. I would guess, due to the great expense Urias had to pay, that your father had been gambling for a long time. The thing about sin is, it blinds us. We don't really see straight. We do things we wouldn't normally do because we have lost our judgment— our ability to understand right from wrong correctly. We justify to ourselves our sinful acts and go on as if the rest of the world is ignorant, or worse."

Prudence thought for a moment. "Father can be rather arrogant," she admitted.

"I imagine your parents love you, and, if you think about it for a bit, you'll remember times of love and joy in your house."

"Yes, there were plenty of those moments when I was younger. It's only been the past two years that they decided I should be married and that my open concern about business matters was not healthy."

Grandma Mac laughed. "Well, forgive the man for those years. You don't want to be starting your marriage with Urias being angry with your parents. Give it to God and leave the nonsense of sin behind you. Your father will one day come to terms with what he's done and is doing.

"Now, enough talk about your father. How are you feeling about getting married in two days?"

"I can't wait," Prudence bubbled out with the answer.

"Wonderful. You've got a good man in Urias. He'll make a good husband."

"He already has been."

"I keep forgetting you're already married."

"In name only. But he's treated me like a wife. Oh, there was a time when he didn't appreciate me because he believed I had conspired with Father. But even during that time, he never said anything or did anything to dishonor me. I know he's a wonderful man. I just hope I can be a good wife to him."

"You will, dear. Just relax and be yourself. That's the person he's fallen in love with." She tapped Prudence on the knee once again and pushed herself up off the log. "I'll leave you be for a spell so you can work out the details with the good Lord about your father. Just remember, God thought him worthy enough to die on the cross for, especially for his shortcomings and sinful nature." Grandma Mac winked.

Prudence watched the old woman take tentative steps down the path toward the smaller house. Prudence thought back on Grandma MacKenneth's parting words. Was she right? Was it as simple as putting Father's sin in perspective as to how God views sin and the sacrifice of the cross?

nineteen

Urias polished the tops of his boots with the back of his trouser legs for the tenth time in as many minutes. He stopped long enough to pace the back room off the sanctuary. Pastor Cloyse had spoken to Urias about ten minutes ago, assuring him that Prudence would be arriving shortly. The last time he peeked, the church was filled with friends. Of course, weddings were a major social event for the small town of Jamestown. Everyone knew everyone else, and all came out.

He'd stayed up half the night, putting some finishing touches on the house, then tossed the rest of the night in anticipation of today. He knew he was making the right decision, yet he still fought the doubts of the past. Thoughts of questioning Prudence's involvement in her father's decisions had poked their ugly heads every fifteen minutes. He countered them with the facts: who Prudence was, how she acted, and how hurt she'd been to learn the truth of her father's ways. Urias knew in his heart she was innocent. He also knew he'd grown to love her and appreciate her.

"Father, bless our marriage," he prayed.

"It's time." Mac poked his head through the doorway. "Ready, Son?"

Urias nodded, unsure of his voice.

His father chuckled and gave him a slap on the back. "The butterflies won't last long. Once you see your bride coming down the aisle, every doubt will fly away."

"Thanks."

"You're welcome. I remember it all too well. Seems to me

there was a young lad who helped set me straight about how much I loved Pam and that I was a fool if I let her get away."

Urias chuckled. "Prudence is a good woman."

"Yes, she is. She'll make you a mighty fine wife."

"Thanks, Dad."

"Pleasure."

The piano music began. Urias took the lead and walked across the front of the sanctuary, taking his position to the left of the pastor and watching for Prudence to come down the aisle. First came Katherine, dressed in a light pink linen dress. She was beautiful with her red curls and green eyes. His heart cried out a silent prayer for his sister. She needed healing, and Urias knew he couldn't heal her. He could only love her and support her in any way possible.

The tempo of the music changed. Urias looked up, and Prudence, in a white dress with a flowing skirt, stood at the entrance of the church sanctuary. Her long brown hair was spun with lace, and the veil covered her face with the slightest of shadow.

His heart skipped a beat. His palms instantly dampened. He started to brush the tops of his boots once again and caught himself just in time.

A smile brimmed from ear to ear. She was beautiful, and she was a gift from the Lord.

Slowly, Prudence made her way down the aisle.

The people in the church seemed to disappear. The only person he saw was Prudence. His gift from God.

"Dearly beloved. . ." The minister began the service. Urias kept his gaze fixed on Prudence. She seemed as nervous as he had been a few moments earlier. He held her hand in his. They faced the pastor and said their vows, dedicating themselves to one another and the Lord.

"You may kiss the bride," the pastor concluded.

Urias lifted the veil and took in her beauty for a moment before closing the gap between them. The kiss was sweet as honey. He pulled back slightly and whispered, "I love you."

"I love you, too," Prudence replied.

They were finally one before God and man. Urias looped his arm and waited for Prudence to place her hand in the crook of his elbow, her touch so intimate, so tender, and so natural. They belonged together. Urias was never more certain of anything in his entire life.

‎❧

Prudence's cheeks ached from smiling.

"Ready?" Urias whispered.

"Yes," she replied. The desire to leave the reception and begin her life as Mrs. Urias O'Leary had peaked an hour ago. The reception was nice, with lots of folks wishing them well. Everyone had brought in food, and Pam and Grandma Mac had even made a three-layered wedding cake. Prudence couldn't ask for a better reception. Apart from wishing her family were here, it was perfect.

Urias flashed his intoxicating green eyes at her and winked. "We'll say our good-byes now."

He took her by the hand and pronounced their departure. A few folks shook their hands, but most just waved them off. The small carriage waited outside the church. A flutter of excitement climbed up her spine as Urias's strong hands went around her waist and helped her step up into the carriage, its narrow bench the perfect setting for an intimate conversation between a man and wife.

Without saying a word, Urias hurried around to the other side and climbed aboard. Taking the leather reins in hand, he snapped them. "Yah."

The carriage lurched forward.

"How are you?"

"Fine."

He placed the reins in one hand, then wrapped her in a loving embrace with his free hand. "I love you, Prudence."

"I love you, too."

He let out a pensive breath.

Prudence leaned her head on his shoulder. "Can you tell me my surprise now?" She'd been wanting to know for weeks what he had been doing in their bedroom.

The lilt of Urias's laughter warmed her. "I hope you're not disappointed."

"How could I be? I don't know what it is."

"Sure you do. It's just our bedroom and the bed I made."

"I know that. But why the big secret?"

He kissed the top of her head. "I don't have much to give you, honey. I had enough to purchase the gold ring, but between building our house and trying to recover from the loss of Bullet, I honestly don't have much money."

"There's always another trip with some hogs."

Urias groaned. "I know. But while I don't have much money, I do have a little talent with wood. Our bedroom and a few of the other final touches on the house are my wedding gift to you."

She sat up straight. "Urias, you've worked so hard. You didn't have to. I would have been content with anything."

"I know that. But it was something I could do. Besides, you're worth it. You're a precious jewel, Prudence, and I wish to honor you with the smaller gifts in the house."

What could she say? She had no gift to give. She had no money, and she had little talent or skills in much of anything. Growing up with servants left one a bit unprepared for the world outside of your own environment.

He turned to look at her. "What's wrong?"

She hesitated for a moment. "I don't have a gift for you."

"You're my gift, honey." He kissed her gently on the cheek.

She cuddled back into his embrace. Could life be better than this? She was in love, and the man she was in love with loved her.

They rounded the bend to the entrance of their new home. It was small, but plenty for the two of them.

"Prudence, there's something we haven't talked about."

A fear of concern tingled up her back. "What's that?"

"Children. I would like to have children. Did you mean it when you told Mrs. Campbell you'd like to have children one day?"

The fear melted. Warmth filled her chest. "Yes, I would like to have children."

"Depending on how the good Lord blesses, I'd like a pack of 'em."

"Pack? Like in wolves?"

"No. Well, a lot of kids, just not wild ones."

Prudence chuckled.

"We're home." He pulled back the reins, then stood to his feet.

He helped her down. Prudence savored the warmth of his hands upon her waist. Then he spun her around in his arms and stepped toward the front door. "May I carry you over the threshold, Mrs. O'Leary?"

O'Leary. It felt right, even though she wasn't from an Irish or Scottish background. She wrapped her arms around his neck and gave a brief nod.

"What would you like to see first?"

"The bedroom." She felt the heat rise on her face. "You've been the most secretive about that room."

"The bedroom it is." Urias carried her through the front door and straight back to the bedroom. "Close your eyes."

"Come on. I've waited this long."

"Shh. Bear with me for a moment longer."

She complied and closed her eyes. She could feel him turning his body to carry her through the doorway. Inside the room, she heard the door close. He set her down. "Keep them closed just a little longer."

Her body shook in anticipation. She could smell a fresh flame burning.

"All right. Open your eyes."

Slowly, she opened them and scanned the room. "Oh, Urias." Her gaze landed on the hand-carved bed. "You did all this?"

"Yes. Do you like it?"

"I love it." She stepped forward, reached out, and touched the smooth surface of the wooden roses carved across the top of the headboard. "It's absolutely beautiful."

"I stained it to simulate a rose color. It's been waxed with five layers."

On the wall were sconces with small mirrors behind the candles. "How could you afford all this?"

"I found an old mirror and cut it up to fit. I used the bits of mirror around the house to enhance the lights. You'll see when you see the rest of the house."

The bed was dressed with a lovely wedding ring quilt. "Who made this?" She fingered the corner.

"Grandma."

Overwhelmed by the old woman's generosity, tears welled in her eyes.

He came up behind her and placed his hands on her shoulders. His breath whispered on her ear. Love flooded around her heart.

"What's the matter?"

"Nothing. I don't deserve this."

"Prudence, you must learn to accept your value in my eyes.

Come here." He led her to the bed and sat down beside her. His thumb lightly brushed away the tear on her cheek. "You are a wonderful person. What happened between your father and myself is in the past. We're married properly now; nothing can change that. I love you and you love me. Nothing else matters."

"I do love you," she confessed. "I think I fell in love with you the moment I met you. At least—the very least—with your green eyes."

Urias chuckled. "Mom was right. She said my wife would adore my eyes."

"You have a wise mother."

"Yes, but I have an equally wise wife. I love you, Prudence. I love who you are, how wise you are with numbers and understanding business. I'm looking forward to our life together. This"—he slowly fanned his hand around the room—"is a small token of the love and appreciation I have for you."

How could a woman ask for more? Prudence leapt into his embrace. She and Urias were beginning their lives as one in God's design. Their lips touched, and completeness filled her. *Thank You, Lord.*

A Letter To Our Readers

Dear Reader:

In order that we might better contribute to your reading enjoyment, we would appreciate your taking a few minutes to respond to the following questions. We welcome your comments and read each form and letter we receive. When completed, please return to the following:

Fiction Editor
Heartsong Presents
PO Box 719
Uhrichsville, Ohio 44683

1. Did you enjoy reading *Hogtied* by Lynn A. Coleman?
   ❏ Very much! I would like to see more books by this author!
   ❏ Moderately. I would have enjoyed it more if

   _____

   _____

   _____

2. Are you a member of **Heartsong Presents**? ❏ Yes ❏ No
   If no, where did you purchase this book? _____

   _____

3. How would you rate, on a scale from 1 (poor) to 5 (superior), the cover design? _____

4. On a scale from 1 (poor) to 10 (superior), please rate the following elements.

   ____ Heroine   ____ Plot
   ____ Hero   ____ Inspirational theme
   ____ Setting   ____ Secondary characters

5. These characters were special because?_____

_____

_____

6. How has this book inspired your life?_____

_____

_____

7. What settings would you like to see covered in future
Heartsong Presents books? _____

_____

_____

8. What are some inspirational themes you would like to see
treated in future books? _____

_____

_____

9. Would you be interested in reading other **Heartsong
Presents** titles? ❏ Yes ❏ No

10. Please check your age range:

❏ Under 18   ❏ 18-24
❏ 25-34   ❏ 35-45
❏ 46-55   ❏ Over 55

Name_____

Occupation _____

Address _____

City_____ State_____ Zip_____

Virginia

4 stories in 1

$\mathscr{S}$panning the innocent age of tall ships through the victory of WWI, this captivating family saga celebrates the rich heritage of Virginia through four romance stories by author Cathy Marie Hake.

Innocence and intrigue, heartbreak and hope mingle in a world where God's grace and the power of love transform lives?

Historical, paperback, 464 pages, 5 ³/₁₆" x 8"

Heartsong

Presents